A Mixed Medicine Bag

Original Black Wampanoag Folklore

Mwalim

"An Oral Tradition in Print"
Atlanta – Boston – New York

Talking Drum Press, LTD
P.O. Box 190028
Roxbury, MA. 02119
talkingdrumpress@gmail.com

© 1995, 1996, 1997, 2007 Mwalim (Morgan James Peters, I)

All rights reserved. No part of this book may be reproduced or transmitted in any form or by any means, electronic, mechanical, including photocopying, recording or by any information storage and retrieval system, without the written permission of the Publisher and/or Author, except where permitted by law. For information address Talking Drum Press, LTD., Roxbury, MA.

Printed in the United States of America

Cover: Russell M. Peters for Wamp Wetu Designs
Interior Photography & Artwork: Mwalim

Library of Congress Cataloging-in-Publication Data

A Mixed Medicine Bag: Original Black Wampanoag Folklore
Au: mjp
Ed: ttkr. sn, ag, bw

ISBN 978-0-9662428-1-2
1. Title
Fiction:
Native American Literature
African American & Multicultural Studies

Dedications:

My Son,
Morgan James Peters, II "Zyggi"
Thanks for letting Daddy test his material on you each night.

My Mother,
Shirley Nurse
Thanks for always telling the most wonderful stories.

My Grandmother,
Gladys Osborne
An inspiration for many tales left to be told.

My Brother,
Randolph G. Peters, Jr.
Yeah, you're in a couple of these stories. (Smile.)

Thank You To:

Ti Kendrick Randall, a dream editor with incredible patience and understanding; Ramona Grant, Wini Noel, Geraldine Thomas, Gail & Kenneth Anderson – for always being there; Lynda Patton & James Spruill for opening many doors; My cousins: Robert Peters, Russell Peters, Hartman & Melanie Deetz, Cedric & Cheryl Cromwell; Edward & Lisa Rhymes; Leslie Lee; John Landry; Earl "Guy" Cash, Jr.; Nancy L. Peters; Eleanor "The Mayor of Main Street" Thaxton – for keeping me in line; Tah Phrum Duh Bush!, Gregory Segarra, Lillian & Herb Segarra – for your on-going encouragement; Juan "J. Golden Eyes" Reyes; Raul Maldonado, the poet warrior; Michael Tritto, Jr.; James Pringle; Michael Shaw – for letting me tell my stories in second grade; Edna Barnett – for making me learn to love reading in sixth grade; Floyd Barbour – for opening eyes and minds; Bronx Writer's Center – for paid gigs; Bronx Council on the Arts – for support; Talking Drum Press Editorial Board (Titi-Tyree, Danny, Alexis, Brian, and Greg) – for kicking it back until it was right; William Hogan; Peter Owens; Charles White; George Smith; New African Company; Oversoul Theatre Collective; Mashpee Wampanoag Tribal Council; Mashpee Wampanoag Elder's Council; Mashpee Wampanoag Rod & Gun Club; Eastern Suns; Wakeby Lake; Live From The Edge Theatre/ The Point CDC; John A. Cole; Lorraine & Jibreel Khazan; Union Lodge #4, Prince Hall Grand Lodge, F&AM; Raymond Coleman; and all of my people from Music & Art/ LaGuardia High School, Boston University, and Goddard College.

Those Who've Joined The Ancestors:

My Grandpa, James N. Osborne; Granddaddy, Allan H. Nurse; Great Uncle & Godfather, Raymond H. Smith; Great-Aunt & Godmother, Gwen Smith; Father, Randolph G. Peters, Sr.; Godfather, Charles Williams; Uncles, John A. Peters, Sr. and Russell M. Peters, Sr.; Cousin, Steven A. Peters, III; Aunt, Clara Kelliinui; Tribal Elders: Mary Lopez, Teddy W. Hendricks, Sr., Ernestine Gray, Rose White-Hughes; Griot Elders: Oscar Brown, Jr., Brother Wayne (X) Grice, Edmund Cambridge, Richard Pryor, August Wilson, Robin Harris, Leroy Thaxton, Lumumba Carson, James Brown, and all of those who helped to clear a path for a young man in a strange world.

A Mixed Medicine Bag

Table of Contents

This is My Folk Tale... A Prologue	1
1. Turtle, The Snakes, & The Drum	7
2. Three Locks of Hair *	11
3. A Rooster's Tale	21
4. Lion's Brew	27
5. The Great Mongoose Rebellion	31
6. Turtle & The Oak Tree	37
7. Backwoods People ♦	43
8. A Lizard Appears	53
9. Rooster & Fox	61
10. A Child Is Born	71
11. The Duet	79
12. Lion's Magic	93
13. The Society Secret	99
14. Yusef's Groove ♦	109
15. A Return to the Backwoods ♦	133

* Inspired by the traditional fairytale, "Three Golden Hairs"
♦ Parental discretion advised for readers/ listeners under 13 years of age.

Walk slowly, breath deeply, and take time to see it all...

A MIXED MEDICINE BAG

THIS IS MY FOLK TALE ... A PROLOGUE

Folklore • *n.* The traditional beliefs, values, stories, customs, and wisdom of a community, passed on by word of mouth.

Folk tale • *n.* A traditional story originally transmitted orally.

- *Oxford Dictionary, Fourth Edition (1995)*

I know the history of a master plan
Where they used stolen labor, to build stolen land
Then got scared and didn't know how to behave
When they saw native people hiding runaway slaves
They were scared we'd get together and uprise
So the next move was of no surprise:
Issuing laws: a Black person's humanity was only three-fifths
And if native co-existed with Africans, their tribes were considered extinct
When a tribe's extinction was the situation, the reservation became another plantation
Born free and raised to be a warrior
was just another thing they tried to take from ya
They knew what would happen as a matter of fact, for your freedom you'd discount being Black but the hair and lips that you tried to hide led the government to say; they'd decide.
- Excerpt from *Guess Who's Rockin' The Party*

It was philosopher/ Hip-hop MC, KRS-ONE who once said that if you don't know who the author [of a book] is, you don't know what you're reading... you don't know what you've read. I have found this to be true. I'm from the east, my people... Marsipee Wonpanaak (Mashpee Wampanoag). My tribe is "By the Lakes" from the nation of the "People of the First Light." My life experience has been a blend of footpaths through the [rapidly disappearing] woods, and swamps of Mashpee and the streets of New York City. It's powwows, street festivals, socials, barbershops, riverbanks, college campuses, lakes, beaches, drum circles, spoken-word events, sweat lodges, bembes, jazz jams, praise and worship sessions, after-hours parties in basements, warehouses, cranberry bogs, and parks that fuel this voice. It's a fact that I grew up in both of my cultures, with a Bajan (Barbados) mother and Mashpee Wampanoag father. Growing up in Bronx, NY and Mashpee, MA, always left me a little too rural to be urban and a little too urban to be rural. This is my folktale.

There's a difference between being a storyteller and a writer. Storytelling is oral and often recited/ recounted from memory, which can cause parts of the story to change from telling to telling. On the other hand, the works of some writers look good on paper, but translate very poorly to the spoken word. It was in fifth grade, while struggling through a book report, that my mother gave me some assistance and advice. She had me tell her what I wanted to say and then had me write it down. "If you can say it, you can write it," she said. I think that was my beginning as a writer.

Conversation was always a major part of my family. The exchange of experiences, observations, events, anecdotes, ideas, dreams, and plans were constant. My elders were folks like civil servants, fishermen, landscapers, social workers, college professors, barbers, writers, retirees playing pool or bowling, bus drivers, musicians, bartenders, theatre artists, veterans, shopkeepers, preachers, hustlers, and poets. I would be grossly remiss if I did not mention the influences of various other cultures and their oral and literary traditions, such as those of the Yiddish/Judaic, Irish, Latino, and Italian American communities with which I interacted while growing up in Bronx, New York. This is my folktale.

My parents met while my father was living in New York and working for the Campbell's Corporation and my mother was looking to buy land in Mashpee to build a summer home (eventually becoming her year-round home). My father's experience was not uncommon; many eastern native people moved to urban areas and became a part of the urban Black community. A lot of second and third-generation "Urban Indians" became an obscure footnote in the inner-city experience.

It was similar for my paternal grandfather. Although he was born and raised in Mashpee, he went to high school in New Bedford, MA. His college and young adult years were spent in Boston, prior to returning to Mashpee and emerging as a leader in the Wampanoag community. In every picture that I ever saw of him, he was wearing a suit and looking very urbane. When he was drafted into WWI, he refused admittance to a white regiment – which is generally where they placed native soldiers. He instead opted to be in a Black unit. In recounting this story, he explained to his children that in this world, if you're not white – you're Black; and the so-called privileged accommodation offered him in no way improved the status of Indians in this society.

When I was a student at Boston University, I used to visit my uncle at his office in the state building. Uncle John was the Commissioner of Indian Affairs for the Commonwealth of Massachusetts; however, most folks knew him as "Slow Turtle" – Supreme Medicine Man of the Wampanoag Nation.

Unlike the romantic concept of consulting with a medicine man while sitting around a fire circle in the woods, our visits took place in a 15-plus-story office building overlooking downtown Boston, a gold domed state house, and the Boston Commons. During these visits, I was told many stories (some of which I didn't understand until years later). I was given the name "Speaking Turtle" and he told me that I should take walks (without my Walkman) in the woods and observe everything around me. Taking his advice, a new vision of the world opened up to me. This is my folktale.

Why does it seem to be popular opinion that native people are the only ethnic group in this society that is not supposed to evolve? Apparently, if we don't look and live the way we did 500 years ago, we no longer exist. The same is true for our storytelling traditions... we are only supposed to tell stories that have been handed down over the generations to be authentic. It is as if the interjection of new or original thoughts and ideas makes it illegitimate, despite the fact that an integral, yet grossly overlooked, common aspect of many storytelling traditions is the creation of new folktales. It remains imperative that we not only reflect on our past, but on our present, as well. Many traditional stories are not appropriate to tell outside of their cultural contexts and communities. However, schools, libraries, and museums often request "authentic" native and/or African tales. Therefore, as an *authentic* Mashpee Wampanoag, who is also of African ancestry, and having been raised in my cultures, hereby certify that all of my tales are *authentic*.

The role of the storyteller is a mixed bag. We are simultaneously entertainers, critics, comedians, poets, satirists, philosophers, fools, anthropologists, sociologists, and tricksters. I believe that if a person learns to tell a good story and then tells it to someone who repeats it to someone else – reality, as we know it, will be irrevocably altered. Actually, most people are natural storytellers; some just consciously make an effort to turn it into a serious hobby or career. One thing is for sure, in the same way that good writers become good readers; good storytellers evolve from being good listeners.

One of the central paradoxes of communication is, *what was said, what was heard,* and *what was meant* rarely ever match, leaving a tremendous gap in much of human communication. Allegory and lore remain the best ways to preserve and communicate the beliefs, values, and experiences of a people as they engage the unconscious mind in bridging the gaps. For example, animal stories are common allegories found in the lore of many cultures. Animals symbolize aspects of our own personalities and emotions. According to Jung (*Man and His Symbols*) and Fromm (*The Forgotten Language*), these symbols trigger responses in our "collective unconscious[1]" (pg. 35), thus communicating to us on both a conscious and subconscious level. The animals also give the story a certain detachment from the people and events that inspired them, making the social and ethical messages of the story the true focus.

For example, "A Lizard Appears," and "Turtle and the Oak Tree" were inspired by a combination of events. It primarily relates to an incident in the 1800's involving Reverend Joseph Amos[2], and Reverend William Appess, a

---

[1] Hall, Calvin; Nordby, Vernon (eds): *A Primer of Jungian Psychology*. New York: New American, 1973

[2] Reverend Amos was a blind preacher and a primary ancestor of the Mashpee Wampanoag tribe, who preached under an oak tree to the Baptist Mashpees after an overseer, Reverend Phineas Fish, barred Wampanoags from attending services in the Mashpee Meetinghouse. (Russell M. Peters, Jr. – Mashpee Wampanoag Oral Historian)

Pequot Methodist Preacher, called "The WoodLot Riots[3]". As storytelling license allows, I also added in touches of such events as: the formation of the Black Panther Party and current issues around racism and dominion affecting the membership of the Sandwich Monthly Meeting (the oldest "Quaker" meeting in New England).

The first edition of this book was published in 1998 as a seven-story chapbook to sell at my storytelling/ spoken-word performances and folklore lectures. Creating this second edition reminds me of producing an album. There is the review and selection of solid material from your repertoire, putting together the arrangements, recording that perfect take of each note and beat, manipulating and tweaking the sound of each track and finding their proper places in the mix. Then you have to sit down and arrange the songs… This book is my literary *What's Going On?* Or maybe it's just a folktale. Welcome to my folktale… Enjoy!!!

Mwalim 7

Mwalim *7)
Morgan James Peters, I – Kuk8tumtunnup (*Speaking Turtle*)
November 21, 2006

---

[3] Amos and Apess drafted and published a formal resolution, protesting the practice of people from a neighboring community, taking resources from Mashpee, while the reverse was illegal. Some Mashpees, led by Apess tried to peacefully enforce this resolution against a group from the neighboring community who were removing firewood from the territory. Despite their non-violence, Apess and several Mashpees were arrested and imprisoned for "riot and assault." Apess was also charged with trespassing, as he did not receive permission from the overseer of the Mashpee territory to live in the district. (ibid)

~ One ~

Turtle, the Snakes and the Drum

Long ago, there were no people – only animals. Well, that's not entirely true. There were people, just not a lot of them; and the few who were around, didn't bother the animals or the woods too much. They all seemed to have a respect for the animals, which the animals appreciated. The people recognized some of the animals as their ancestors, which the animals also appreciated. Then, the people and the animals could understand each other. Nowadays, people don't even understand people.

In the land where there are now malls, golf courses and condominiums, there used to be just woods, lakes and swamps. In the woods, things flowed on a mellow vibe and the balance of nature was even. The turtles lived in the place where the swamp met the woods, among the soft moss and the roots of the trees. Turtles looked very different in those days. In fact, turtles looked a lot like lizards. In fact, no one could tell the difference between a lizard and a turtle, except for one animal: the snake. You see, a turtle was a snake's favorite food – next to chicken. Since there were no chickens in the woods, this kinda left turtles as the snake's number one delicacy. Since turtles were smart creatures, they made sure that they remained a delicacy, a rare meal for a snake, or a snake's family.

One thing about snakes; they hate drums. Drums annoy them and give them headaches. They also believed that drums would make the more passive animals rebel, so whenever they heard a drum, their paranoia would set in and they would slither away from the sound. There were many times when snakes would lobby the congress of nature to make drums illegal (but that's another story). Because they were patient and slow learners who took their time to understand what they were doing, turtles could get the most amazing sounds out of a drum. Turtles would give each beat a meaning, while other animals would just beat on the drums for the sake of banging. For many animals, the drums were just amusing instruments. The raccoons, in particular, thought that they were slick because they had opposing digits and could do pseudo thumb slides on the drums. For turtles, drums were living things.

The one thing that could protect a turtle from a snake was a drum, so turtles started carrying their drums with them. Whenever they saw a snake coming, they would start to play their drums to drive them back. They also started using the drum to communicate over great distances, carrying on conversations with each other from miles away. After a while, some of the snakes lost heart and became vegetarians. Others took to preying on insects and rodents, which nobody seemed to mind, on account of there being too many of them anyway. Yeah, it began to look like the turtles had won that round.

Some of the snakes were rather stubborn and vindictive. They hated turtles simply because they were turtles. Now mind you, these snakes didn't know why they hated turtles; they just knew that they hated turtles because their parents hated turtles, just as their parent's parents hated turtles, and so on. The really funny thing about these snakes was that they looked like they had a little turtle in them, especially around the eyes, nose and mouth. Every now and again, you would even catch one of them bobbing their head to the beat of a turtle's drum. Then they would realize what they were doing and begin to hiss and spit in disgust over the "obscene turtle noise."

One evening, a young turtle was walking up the road with his drum. The sun was setting behind him as he made his way through the woods. Now what this young turtle didn't know was that a group of these turtle-hating snakes had decided that they were going to ambush the first turtle that came by. Then the snakes set about plugging their ears with clay so that the drum wouldn't bother them. Anyway, along came this turtle singing a little turtle song to himself that has long since been forgotten. (You see, years later, snakes took over the woods and started passing laws that only their history and culture would be recorded).

The snakes saw the turtle coming and began to surround him, slithering out from all sides of the road. The young turtle began to play his drum, but the snakes kept coming. He kept playing his drum until he saw that it wasn't stopping the snakes. Suddenly, the turtle got an idea and climbed up into the drum. He knew that the snakes wouldn't come after him in there because they were afraid of the body of the drum and the sounds that came out of it. The snakes, being rather stubborn creatures, decided that they would wait. They figured that the turtle would have to come out sometime. It began to rain, but the snakes waited. The weather turned cold, but the snakes waited. It got windy, and the snakes waited. It began to snow… the snakes caught some terrible colds and to this day, a snake still can't smell through his nose, only his tongue.

As for the turtle, when the drum sensed the turtle's fear, it began to hug him as a means of offering protection from the snakes. Remember, drums come from trees and trees come from the earth, and the earth nurtures and heals all things. So that's how the turtle got his shell.

One evening, a young turtle was walking up the road with his drum. The sun was setting behind him as he made his way through the woods...

~ Two ~

Three Locks of Hair

In an African kingdom, up in the Northeastern part of the continent, there was a small village. In the village, a young woman was giving birth to a child. The people of the village had been waiting for this birth for quite some time, as it had been prophesied many years before. Now, prophesied births were nothing new to this region; but, this happened to be one that the villagers were quite eager to see come to pass.

It was a difficult birth for the mother. After several agonizing hours, she gave birth to a boy. After the birth, the old midwife went to the door of the house and told the people outside, "Another ancestor has returned. It is a boy..." The crowd was happy to hear the news. "Is it the baby that we have been expecting?" asked one of the men in the crowd. "He has the birthmark on his left arm: an eight-pointed sun, a crescent moon and five-pointed star." responded the midwife. The crowd grew loud with delight. At last, the baby who would become king was born. He would become the benevolent king who would change the laws of the land. The midwife raised her hands and hushed the crowd. "You are disturbing a new mother and child!" The crowd disbanded and as they walked away, they chatted about what wonderful changes this king would bring to the land. Many spoke of how fortunate they were that he would come from their village. They each talked about the roles that they would play in the child's' upbringing.

As morning turned to evening, a happy event quickly turned into a sad one. The mother died, leaving the child parentless. His father had died in a hunting accident. The discussion in the crowd became one of, "I wonder who's going to take care of the poor infant?" Among the crowd, listening and not talking, was Amin – the current king's advisor. He had been traveling a great distance and was on his way back to the king when he stopped into this village to rest. While in the village, he had heard the details of the prophecy of the child who would become the next king. It was said that by his Knowledge-Build degree (eighteenth year), he would take over the kingdom and take the king's daughter as his wife.

Amin knew that the king would not be pleased to hear this. He immediately returned to the palace to deliver the news and gained an audience with Hassan, the king. Hassan was not pleased to hear this news and was even less happy with the solution that Amin proposed. "We should go to the village and offer to adopt the child. We could give the child the best of care..." Amin said.

"Are you insane?" interrupted Hassan. "Take the child in and raise him? If my wife gives birth to a daughter, he will be around her... what are you thinking?"

Amin cleared his throat, took a deep breath and said, "You haven't heard the whole idea. We will take the child, put him in a box and drop the box into the river." This, Hassan thought, was a marvelous idea. That night, they started out for the village. By the next day, they had the baby, placed him in a wooden box, and had thrown him into the river. Because the box was made of a light wood it floated.

For some reason, placing babies in boxes and floating them down a river was not all that unusual in this region. People discovering a box in the river and being delighted at the finding, also wasn't that unusual. This time around, there was a young couple in the southern part of the region that had a small farm next to the river. The wife, Isha, was tending the fields and her husband, Mustafa, was repairing the canals that fed water into his fields. The wife spotted the box when it got stuck in the branches of a tree that had fallen into the river. She called to her husband, who waded out to the box, pulled it from the branches, and carried it onto the shore. They opened the box and were delighted to find a baby in it. Isha had discovered a year before that she could not have children and was excited that this would be their son. The wife noticed the sun, moon and star on the baby's left arm and decided to name him Faruq. Faruq grew from a strong, healthy baby into a strong, healthy boy and then a strong, healthy teenager.

As the years passed, the king and his advisor took to traveling a lot to other kingdoms. The king needed to borrow money from these other kingdoms because his supply of gold was diminishing. As fate would have it, King Hassan and Amin were traveling to a kingdom that was to the southwest of their own. This trip took them past a small farm next to the river. The farm was approximately two days away from the palace and another two days away from their destination. The travelers decided to stop there for the night and continue on their journey in the morning. It was the habit of King Hassan to travel in disguise so that if he stopped in a village, he would not be recognized. It was not out of humility that he did this; he just didn't want his subjects to know that he was traveling to other countries for gold. What kind of king needs to borrow?

On this night, Mustafa, Isha and Faruq were celebrating Faruq's discovery day. Since they didn't know his birthday, they could only go by the day that he was found in the box. They didn't want to deceive Faruq and Faruq believed that he never could have loved his real parents more. Mustafa answered the door and welcomed two visitors into his home; unaware that this was King Hassan and his advisor, Amin. He invited them to join their little celebration and to partake of food and wine. The visitors gratefully accepted. Over dinner, there was pleasant conversation and the two travelers told tales of the many journeys they'd made. They both took an instant liking to Faruq, who was a polite young man. Faruq commented that he wanted to travel when he got older and see some of the world. "You may just do that," said King Hassan, as he drained his wine cup.

Faruq, having been raised to be a good host, got up to pour more wine into his guest's cup. While he poured the wine, his sleeve fell back and his birthmark was revealed. King Hassan and Amin stared at it, as if hypnotized. "Is there something wrong?" asked Mustafa.
"Oh, uh, no..." responded Amin, "we couldn't help but notice that, uh, interesting tattoo on your son's arm."

Mustafa and Isha looked at each other, "It's not a tattoo, it's a birthmark, Sir." Said Isha. King Hassan rose to his feet and turned slightly pale (especially noticeable since everyone in the kingdom was rather dark).

"That is quite a birthmark." said Amin, as he guided the king back to his seat. Amin changed the subject slightly, giving King Hassan enough of a chance to regain his composure. He had been sitting here, being entertained and charmed by the very young man who it was prophesied would take over his kingdom, this very year. He thought that he had done away with this child years ago. How could he pop up again so many years later? He had to think of a way to eliminate the young man, but how?

Finally, after more wine and conversation, the king had become quite drunk. The sweet wine made by the villagers was much more potent than the fine wine served at the palace. Amin had an idea, he stood up and raised his cup as if in a toast, "You are too kind, all of you. It is time that we reveal who we are. This is King Hassan and I am the Royal Advisor, Amin. We are on a mission of great importance to the kingdom. Amin reached into his belt and removed a small purse of gold. The family, who had all dropped to their knees when they found out that they were in the presence of the king, refused to accept the gold. Amin insisted that they take it and asked if Faruq would be willing to perform an important errand for them. Of course Faruq was willing to do what ever they asked; he had been raised to respect the king.

Amin took a scroll from his bag along with a pen and some ink. He wrote a message on the cloth scroll, had the king sign it, rolled it and gave it to Faruq. "Take care not to read this, for it is a secret message that you carry. You are to take this to the palace and deliver it. Faruq and his family were honored that the king had given him such responsibility. His mother packed a travel bag for Faruq and he started off for the palace the next morning. The King and Amin resumed their journey to the next kingdom.

Along the way, Faruq grew tired. He went to the door of an old house and knocked – hoping that they would allow him rest in their stable. In the house lived an old woman and her two elderly brothers. They invited Faruq in for dinner and to stay the night. During dinner, one of the brothers noticed his birthmark. Knowing the prophecy, he instantly felt honored to have this young man in his house and assumed that the young man, who looked to be about in his knowledge-god (17th) or Knowledge-Build (18th) degree, was on his way to become the king. That night, when Faruq fell asleep, the scroll fell out of his bag and fell open. The eldest brother read it. He called to his brother and sister and told them what the scroll said:

When this young man reaches the palace have the guards take him and execute him immediately. Have his remains fed to the vultures.

The eldest brother was a poor, righteous teacher who had understanding of many things. He knew the truths of life and taught them to whoever sought knowledge, wisdom and understanding. He knew that there was a reason that this young man ended up at his door and that the mathematics of the universe decided that he would be the one to help this young man bring the prophesy to fruition. He had many scrolls in his side room; he found one that looked like the king's and forged a new note in Amin's handwriting and with the king's signature. The new scroll read:

When this young man reaches the palace, he is to be given new clothes, and is to immediately be married to the princess.
All Praises,
 King Hassan

The brother then took the new scroll and placed it in the bag. The next morning, Faruq had breakfast with the family.
"Do you know who you are?" asked the eldest brother.
"I am Faruq, son of Mustafa and Isha, Sir."
"Ah, but do you have knowledge of self?" the eldest brother inquired further.
"I guess I don't know what you mean, Sir."
The eldest brother smiled and said "When you are finished your journey, come back and I will teach you. These are things that you will need to know in the future." After breakfast, Faruq thanked them and resumed his journey to the palace.

Upon reaching the palace, he handed the scroll to the captain of the guards. The captain read the scroll and escorted Faruq to the Queen, who read the scroll and was overjoyed. She sent for her daughter, a lovely young woman named

Nahima, and she was immediately married to Faruq. Their honeymoon lasted for 30 nights.

On the thirty-first day, King Hassan and Amin return to the palace to find Faruq very much alive and happy with his daughter. He was outraged! How could this have happened? He didn't write the scroll that his wife handed him, but who did? Amin sat calmly and said to Faruq, "So, you have found your bride! But, you are not yet ready to call yourself the crown prince. You must earn that honor." Faruq said that he was ready for whatever was necessary. King Hassan, following his advisor's lead, smiled and said, "You are to go to Pelan where you will find the mountains. In the mountains live savage giants. You are to bring me three locks of hair from the head of a giant." Faruq, not understanding the danger, agreed and set off on his journey, in spite of his bride imploring him not to go. She understood that this journey would mean his death.

Faruq crossed into the land of Pelan and could see the mountains in the distance. He had heard of Pelan and how a madman had grafted[4] some terrible beings called "devils" in this land. These devils were the savage giants that Hassan spoke of.

Halfway into Pelan, Faruq came to a great stone gate. At the gate stood a large, muscular Black man with a tremendous sword and piles of skulls at his feet. Faruq asked if he could pass through and the man allowed him passage. After Faruq passed through the gate, the man told him that he would not be able to pass back, unless he could answer a riddle. If Faruq failed to answer the riddle and tried to leave, the man would have to behead him. Faruq asked for the riddle and the man directed him to the center of a circle where two lines

---

[4] Grafting in this sense is a scientific process of selecting males and females from a given species with particular genetic characteristics for breeding purposes. This process often involves in-breeding.

intersected. On the end of one line, at the edge of the circle in front of Faruq, sat a rock. To his right sat a flute; behind him sat a stick; to his left was a glazed clay jar filled with water. The man then asked, "If the rock is the earth, the flute is the wind, the stick is fire and the jar is the ocean, what are you?" Faruq sat in the middle of the circle and thought for a long time. He then said that he would give the man the answer when he returned.

Between Faruq and the mountains was a great lake to cross. The water was green and foul smelling. The only way across lake was to use a ferry, paddled by a ferryboat man. He was an old man, attached to the boat by heavy looking chains. At first, the man refused to take him across. However, when he saw Faruq's birthmark he said, "I'll take you across if you can find some way to release me from this boat. I was chained here by one of the giants many years ago. Faruq agreed to help him and the old man paddled him across the lake to the mountains.

On the banks of the lake, Faruq saw an old woman who looked strangely familiar. He called out to her and she looked up as if startled. As they spoke and he explained his task, she noticed the mark on his arm. Suddenly, she began to laugh and clap her hands. At last, the prophecy was coming true! The old woman had been the midwife who brought Faruq into the world. The giants had long ago captured her. Normally, they would have killed her; however, they knew that she possessed great wisdom and they chose to keep her as a slave. She knew that Faruq would be coming eventually, and knew the whole story.

She explained that the king was trying to have him killed because he did not want to give up the throne. He believed that he would live forever because he had been given the lessons of life. The king had made laws that made it illegal for common people to be educated, thus, cutting them off from the truths and mathematics of the universe. She took Faruq back to the cave that her master lived in and hid him behind a rock. She then started to make dinner for the giant. The giant was the envy of all of his friends because he had somebody who knew the secret of cooking meat.

The giant returned to his cave and was greeted by the old woman. She then started to say, "I had an interesting dream last night. I dreamt that an old man was chained to a ferryboat and didn't know how to free himself." The giant laughed as he heard this and said, "I know somebody who did that to an old man. The only way that the old man can be free is to drop his paddle and have someone riding in the boat catch it. When this happens, he'll be free and they'll be chained! Hee, hee, hee, heee!!!" The old woman then looked at the giant in such a fashion that made the giant ask, "What's wrong?"

"Oh, nothing. When was the last time you let me fix your hair?"

"My hair," responded the giant, "what's wrong with my hair?"

"It could use a little washing, combing, clipping...."

"Well then, get to it!!" Responded the giant.

The old woman washed his hair with a mix of herbs, combed it and started trimming it. The giant loved it. With her clipper, she cut off three locks of hair and dropped them under her apron. By the time she was finished, the giant had fallen into a deep sleep.

Faruq came out of his hiding place and took the locks of hair. He thanked the old woman and was about to leave when an idea hit him. "Come with me." he said. Without a word, the old woman left the cave with him and made her way down the side of the mountain where the ferryboat was waiting. The ferry took them across the lake and Faruq turned to the old man and said, "The next time you have a passenger, drop your paddle. When they catch it, they'll be chained to the boat and you'll be free." The old man thanked him. When Faruq and the old woman reached the stone gate, the guard asked him for the answer to the riddle. Faruq had remembered an old tale that his adopted father told him where God was always positioned at the center of the elements. Faruq took a deep breath and said, "If the rock is earth, the flute is air, the stick is fire, the jar is the ocean, then I am God." The guard took a deep breath, dropped his sword and said, "You both may pass." Faruq and the old woman made their way out of Pelan and returned to the palace.

Upon seeing Faruq and the three locks of hair, King Hassan was outraged. Amin was completely stumped. How could this young farm-boy have outsmarted him? Faruq took this opportunity to tell the king, "Sir, you will be happy to hear this. The mountain is covered with gold! The ground was gold and the caves were filled with gold! I know that you are looking for gold, so I thought you would like to know." King Hassan's outrage turned into joy at this news. He decided that he and Amin would start off for Pelan in the morning. "Oh yes, one thing, Sir", said Faruq, "You will need to take a ferryboat across a lake. An old man paddles it and he is kind of weak. If he drops an oar, be sure to catch it." King Hassan said that he would be careful. The next morning he and Amin left the palace and were never heard from again. It is rumored that Amin now serves the giant of the mountain.

Faruq summoned the elderly, poor, righteous teacher and his parents to the palace. The old midwife and the poor, righteous teacher became his advisors. Within a degree, Faruq had knowledge of self and knew the mathematics of the universe. Faruq and his descendants ruled the kingdom for three hundred and sixty years, opening many schools and libraries throughout the kingdom. For the first time (and possibly, the only time) knowledge was considered gold.

~ Three ~

A Rooster's Tale

Many years after the turtle got his shell, animals began to find that their spirituality was separating from them. Once upon a time, their spirits were one with the world around them, but as time went on things became more complex. Suddenly, the animals could no longer find their spirits in the grass, trees, rivers, fields and skies.

The animals began to look elsewhere for their spirits, not realizing that their spirits had never left them. Some of the animals maintained a relationship and connection with the spiritual world and often had visions that they shared with the other animals. Sometimes they could "see" the spirits of the other animals and interpret the spirit's message. These animals became known as "spiritual leaders."

Some of these spiritual leaders were legitimate. They would help and counsel any animal that came to them, asking for nothing in return and occasionally getting just that – nothing. Sometimes, a thankful animal would make a generous donation of food or goods to the spiritual leader, but usually the spiritual leaders made their living doing something else.

Some animals, however, saw this as an opportunity to make a living. Many of them had no more of an idea of how to connect with their spirits than the animals who came to them for advice. One of these spiritual leaders was an arrogant, loud and rude animal called Rooster. Rooster used to strut around with his chest sticking out, looking down his no... I mean *beak*, at everybody who walked by. He would also brag about the fact that he had twenty women at his beck and call and several children by each of them. Rooster had a suave and slick manner which many animals found appealing. They mistook his smooth ways for a sign that he was the chosen one and they should follow him.

Once a week, Rooster began holding big meetings where he would help animals to "reconnect with their souls". Three or four times during the meeting, he would have the animals donate food and other goods for his services. He said that their spirits wanted this and that it was the right thing to do. He said that if they did not comply, their spirits would be unhappy and the animals would never see them again. Sometimes animals would barely have enough food for themselves, but Rooster would tell them, "Being hungry is a small price to pay for being with your own spirit..." The animals would hand over all that he requested.

After a while, Rooster got the animals to build a big meetinghouse for him to hold meetings in. It was a big, fancy room with a beautiful house attached for Rooster to live in. The meeting hall was within fifty yards of the coop/shack that his 20 hens and 275 offspring lived in. Rooster lived very well from the donations that the animals made to him and he soon grew really fat. The donations that he couldn't use, he either sold to the animal store wholesale or traded for silk suits and gold pocket watches. It could be said that Rooster was not conceited, but convinced.

Rooster also developed a hustle where he opened a store that sold trinkets and charms to help animals find good luck and fortune in their lives. Animals were buying red yarn to place on their windowsills, wooden sticks to put under seats and pillows, and powders to sprinkle at the entrances to their homes.

Rooster prided himself on his singing voice. During meetings, he would preach and then burst into crowing a song. The chickens in the front row would all swoon when he did this; the other animals found it annoying. "That bird's cackle could wake the dead!" complained one of the elder spiritual leaders (who did his work for free). They felt that something needed to be done about Rooster because he was making a mockery of a serious and sacred position in the community. There had to be some way to teach him a lesson... they thought and thought until Owl came along.

Owl's hobby was astronomy because he stayed awake all night and flew around. He knew the position of the stars and planets and the motion of the earth. He told the spiritual leaders that there was going to be a full eclipse of the sun in twelve days. The eclipse was going to last all day until 4:00 PM. Shifting their attention away from dealing with Rooster, the spiritual leaders listened to this news. Suddenly, Raccoon started laughing and clapping his paws together. The other leaders asked him what was going on. He stopped laughing long enough to say, "I know how we can deal with Rooster! Listen to this..." He shared his idea with the other animals and they agreed that it was a good one. They made arrangements to meet again the next week to talk about the plan further.

The next week, the spiritual leaders went to Rooster's house and knocked on the door. A young chicken let them in and led them into Rooster's den where they had a seat and were offered cold drinks. Rooster came out, dressed in a smoking jacket, with an ascot around his neck and a pipe in his beak. He greeted the leaders in his characteristically pompous fashion and took a seat in his recliner.

Speaking Turtle was the spokesman; he was the only one who could deal with the arrogant Rooster without getting mad. "We have come to tell you that our spirits tell us that the sun is angry with you. Beginning tomorrow, the sun wants you to greet him early every morning with a song or he will not rise again." Rooster's eyes opened wide in surprise. He looked around the room, studying the faces of the animals, and then laughed. "You expect me to believe a story like that? The sun will rise tomorrow like he always does. I'm not getting up early in the morning for anything or anybody, not even the sun..." he replied. The animals tried to reason with him but Rooster wouldn't hear any of it. He excused himself, left the room, and asked the chicken to show them all out.

Rooster never did like to get up early. His weekly meetings began at two in the afternoon, allowing him to sleep in until 1:00 PM. The next morning, Rooster woke up to complete darkness. He figured that he had awakened too early until he lay in bed for a while and his body told him that it was at least 11:30 in the morning. He got up and found breakfast waiting for him. He looked out the window and saw the animals going on with their daily business, like they do every day – except it was as dark as night outside.

After a couple of hours, Rooster began to panic. What if he really had offended the sun? Would the sun ever forgive him? He got dressed and went to see Speaking Turtle. Now Rooster never went to visit anyone unless he wanted something. He felt that visiting animals was beneath him. If they wanted to be social, they knew where his house was. Anyway, he went to Speaking Turtle who was expecting him. He found the turtle sitting in his den playing chess with his cousin, Lizard. Rooster asked Speaking Turtle for advice and Turtle sat very quiet for a few seconds and looked at the ceiling (as was his way when he was deep in thought). Finally, he cleared his throat and said, "First, you're going to have to give up all of your wealth." "Are you crazy?", sputtered Rooster, I'm not giving it up for anything!!" Speaking Turtle focused his attention back on the chessboard, "It's just as well; you'll need all that grain of yours to store up. With no sunlight, no new crops are going to grow." Rooster thought for a minute, and then relented, "Okay. What else?" Turtle stared at the ceiling again. "You are going to have to sing to him every morning, and dedicate your weekly meetings to him, from now on." Rooster thought for a minute, "Okay. I'll do it!" Turtle looked at the ceiling again, "He wants you to prove it and sing to him right now, from the highest place in the land." With that, Rooster got up, ran outside, flew to the top of the tallest tree and started singing with all of his might. The moon began to move, and the sunlight flooded the earth in its warm glow.

Rooster gave up his fancy house and moved back into the coop with his wives and children, which wasn't really so bad. At least there, as the only rooster for 25 hens and 331 chicks, he was still the man... or bird as it were. The days of his weekly meetings were called Sun-day and every morning a rooster will stand on a high perch and sing his greeting to the sun.

"We have come to tell you that our spirits tell us that the sun is angry with you. Beginning tomorrow, the sun wants you to greet him early every morning with a song or he will not rise again."

~ Four ~

LION'S BREW

When the creator put animals on the earth, each of them was assigned responsibilities. Lion, and his cat cousins, were given the task of ruling all living things on the earth. They roamed the jungles, mountains, forests and plains of the planet, making sure that things didn't get out of hand. Lion was basically a good-natured soul. He was a vegetarian and looked out for the general health and well-being of the animals. He had strong lungs and when he roared, it could be heard for miles around. There were a few people, who lived among these animals, but they didn't bother the animals and the animals didn't bother them.

Lions, like most cats, liked lying in the sun, napping and occasionally taking a bath or giving one to another lion. The other animals didn't have a problem with this arrangement and nature was properly balanced – everything and everyone was able to co-exist peacefully. However, way up in the north, there were some large, hairy ape-like creatures that roamed the earth, lived in caves, and ate meat. They had also learned how to summon and use fire. These creatures wanted to rule all living things on the earth and decided that they would need to defeat Lion, if they ever hoped to assume his position.

Their first idea was to kill Lion, until one of them realized that Lion would be very useful to them in the future. Lion had senses and instincts that they did not possess, not to mention the respect of all of the other animals on the earth. On the other hand, the other animals laughed at them and ran from them whenever they came near. They came to realize that the way to defeat Lion would be to gain control of him. If they could gain control of Lion, they would have the respect of all of the other animals on the earth. Now the problem became *how* they would gain control of Lion. They thought and thought until an idea finally came to them. They were watching some small cats playing with the leaves of a plant. As they continued to play with the leaves, they got a little sillier and would roll on their backs and claw at the sky. The ape-like creatures realized that the leaves must have some power to make the cats behave that way.

Some of the ape-like creatures picked a bunch of leaves from one of the bushes that the cats were playing in, placed them in a big clay pot of water and put the pot over a fire. The water began to boil and the leaves began to brew. They let the water boil for two days, adding more water every so often. Finally, they took the pot off of the fire, added honey to it and let it cool in the ice and snow outside of their cave. When the brew was cold, they took the pot down into the jungle. When the animals and the people saw them coming, all but Lion ran and hid in the woods. Lion was not afraid of anyone or anything. The ape-like creatures were very friendly and told Lion that they had made a special drink just for him – a brew fit only for the king of the earth.

Lion smelled the pot and the aroma was delicious. He stuck his head in the pot and took a long drink. Suddenly, he felt really giddy and began laughing and prancing around. He spun round and round in a circle until he got quite dizzy and fell backward into the grass, laughing, purring, and clawing at the sky. After a while, when the effects of the brew wore off and he wanted some more, the ape-like creatures gave it to him. By the third or fourth time he had this brew, he was unable to imagine living without it. The feeling that it gave him was unlike anything he'd ever felt before. He went back to the pot, but it was empty. "Can you make some more of that brew for me?" asked Lion. The ape-like creatures smiled at each other and then at him and said, "Well, we could, if only..." Lion was nearly frantic, "If only what?" he asked.

"If only we had more land to grow the plant from which this brew is made."

"How much land do you need?"

"Oh, not much, just enough to grow about 10 or 15 fields of the plants."

Lion's eyes grew big as he imagined fields of these marvelous plants growing in his jungle. He agreed and they began clearing out sections of the jungle to start their crops. Up until that point, the animals and people had been able to hide in its rich green foliage. Of course, in clearing the jungle, the ape-like creatures were able to capture some of the people and kill and eat many of the animals who lived in there.

Lion began having this brew every day and spent less and less time taking care of the earth and more and more time prancing and rolling on the ground, enjoying the feeling that the brew gave him. Every so often, the supply of the brew would fall off and each time Lion would want to know why. The ape-like creatures would tell him that it was because they didn't have enough fields and Lion would give them more land. Pretty soon, these ape-like creatures controlled most of the earth.

One afternoon while Lion was nodding out after his dose of brew, some of the ape-like creatures had an idea. They figured that if they added a little of their blood to the brew, it would make Lion their slave in the same way that the brew captured him. That evening, they gave Lion brew mixed with the blood. All of a sudden, Lion started snarling and roaring. His eyes took on a fiery glaze and he began pacing around the ape-like creatures. Finally, he came to a stop and froze in one place, setting his gaze on one of them. The ape-like creatures watched him in terror. Then, Lion leaped on the ape-like creature that he had been watching and began to eat him. You see, these ape-like creatures were crafty but not very smart. What they had given Lion was a taste for blood, a taste more intense than his desire for the brew. In fact, he lost his taste for the brew and now only wanted blood.

The ape-like creatures scattered back into the mountains, not to be seen again for many years. Some say that they are still trying to find brews that will help them gain control of the earth. However, every time they invent a brew that they think will give them control, the scheme backfires and they are left searching for a cure to save themselves.

To this day, Lion still roams the jungles, mountains, forests and plains looking for animals and blood and cats still play with catnip.

~ Five ~

The Great Mongoose Rebellion

There was a tropical island that had snakes, monkeys and people – in that order. On a tropical island, all kinds of plants and fruits can grow with little effort and these islands were places of great beauty. The people on the island were able to live there with minimal disturbance to the rest of nature. Then some other people in boats came to the island, leveled most of the plants, chased the monkeys away, killed and enslaved the people who were already there and decided to grow fields and fields of plants that they could not grow in their own lands because of the climate.

The people who came over in the boats found that the "natives" made horrible slaves; they kept dying or running away into the jungles. When this happened, the folks with the boats got into their vessels and traveled to two different lands to capture and bring back new slaves, as well as, mongooses (or is it mongeese?). The people who came on the boats were also having trouble with the snakes. They, their families, and the livestock were being bitten and the snakes would eat their crops. The new slaves would be made to work the fields that the boat folks felt that they, themselves, were too important to work.

Unfortunately, they would use the same size boats to bring over the slaves and the mongeese (mongooses?) and stuffed as many slaves in the boats as they did mongooses (mongeese?). As a result, fewer slaves survived the trip than mongeese (mongooses?). The boat people planned to have the mongooses or mongeese clear out the snakes. Their plan worked. As the slaves cleared the fields, the mongooses or mongeese cleared out the snakes. You see, snakes were mongeese's (or is it mongoose's?) favorite food.

The boat people found that the slaves were more useful than the mongeese (or mongooses) because the mongeese (mongooses) had already fulfilled their purpose. Although the boat people made their money as planters, they knew much more about money than they did about soil composition. Some of the slaves that came from a farming culture tried to tell them that their fields were too big – but, the boat people figured that the slaves were just being lazy and made them plant fields all the way to the edge of the island.

Some of the land was on big cliffs and hills and had big trees that needed to be cut down. The slaves knew that when you cut down trees on a hill, near a cliff, you weaken the soil. If you weaken the soil, you weaken the ground. As a result, entire sections of farms began to fall into the ocean.

The slaves were not as lazy as the boat people were dumb. There was also a supply and demand problem that the boat people had not recognized. Because of the rich growing conditions, the crops of tobacco, sugar cane and other warm weather plants were plentiful. Plentiful crops are not always such a good thing – too much product lowers the demand, thus lowering the price.

Now, most of the slaves were no longer useful so the boat people began to consider the slaves, as well as the mongeese (mongooses) to be a *problem*. The way that some of the boat people decided to deal with the problem was to free the slaves and the mongeese (mongooses); give up farming; and go back to where they came from, leaving the newly freed slaves to fend for themselves. Some of the boat people stayed behind and decided that the slaves would need training and structure in order to care for themselves. So, using extreme physical and mental cruelty as educational tools, they taught the ex-slaves to read, write and run a country. This made the ex-slaves less of a nuisance, but the mongooses (mongeese?) were still a problem. Since there were no more snakes, the mongooses began eating the boat people's chickens (chicken tastes a lot like snake).

Mongeese (Mongooses) were trainable animals and some of the planters would keep a mongoose as a pet. One day, a young boat person's boy was given a mongoose as a pet. The mongoose's slave name became Cyril. Although his real name was "Sctitcheeeee" in mongoose, that's hard to pronounce so we'll call him Cyril. Anyway, Cyril became the boy's constant companion, going everywhere the boy went. Together they would run and play around the farm and when the boy went somewhere with his father or one of the servants, Cyril would travel on his shoulders.

In a year, the boy was ready to go to school and during first two days of school, the boy missed Cyril terribly. He started sneaking Cyril to school with him in his inside jacket pocket. Even though they were in the tropics, people wore heavy wool jackets to work and school just like they did in the old country (the boat people's old country, not the slaves). From the boy's pocket, Cyril learned to read, write and do mathematics. The lesson that Cyril enjoyed the most was history, where he learned about governmental structure and parliament. There was one thing that confused Cyril about history; when the teacher was referring to somebody from the boat people's history that did some deed, they were called heroes. However, if someone from another group did the same thing (possibly against the boat people), they were called savages, terrorists or rebels.

Cyril lived a pretty good life. Many of the other mongooses (mongeese?) were being captured and killed for stealing chickens from the farmers. He thought that this was unfair since the farmers had more than enough chickens for themselves and were being just plain selfish. After all, the mongeese were perfectly happy in their old country where there were lots of snakes. It was the boat people's fault that they were in this new land in the first place. It wasn't the mongeese's fault that the island ran out of snakes (resulting in a growth in the population of mosquitoes and other insects – but that's another story).

A lot of the local farms had mongeese (mongooses) as pets. One night, after everybody was asleep, Cyril snuck out and went around to the other farms, calling the other mongooses (mongeese) to come out for a meeting. The mongeese came together for their meeting in secret. Since mongooses could be owned, they thought that they were under the same laws as the slaves used to be, which meant that they could not meet or speak in their native language. Cyril and the other mongeese talked about the plight of their brothers, sisters and cousins who were facing starvation or death at the hands of the planters.

The first order of business was for the domestic mongeese (or... well, you get the idea) to be educated. Cyril was able to achieve this within twelve meetings. The next order of business was to bring in the wild mongooses (mongeese?) and educate them; this was achieved in another twelve meetings. Then they set up a governmental structure that used *Robert's Rules of Order* (which they stuck to very closely). After 120 meetings, the mongeese of the island were ready to break away and form their own nation. On the first full moon after their last meeting, all of the domestic mongooses (mongeese) left their homes and joined the wild ones in the hills of the island.

Now, the servants of the planters had a special place in their hearts for the mongeese (mongooses) and would leave the doors to the chicken coops and kitchens open. They had a deal with the mongeese (mongooses) that the mongooses (mongeese) would only take the food they needed. In return, the mongeese (mongooses) would teach them how to set up a government and break away from the rule of the boat people's country.

Every now and again, by the light of the full moon, you will see several small creatures slink down out of the hills and onto the farms and plantations. As these creatures would sneak back into the hills, dragging things with them, voices from the servant's quarters could be heard softly singing:

Sly mongoose
Don't know your name
Sly mongoose
Cry out for shame
Sneak up into the white man's kitchen
Eat up all of the fat roast chicken
And they know there's no use tricking
Sly mongoose

Once a week, when the turtle sat under the oak tree, he would speak. He'd tell stories and share his visions with anyone who might have been around

~ Six ~

Turtle & The Oak Tree

Have you ever sat under an oak tree? I mean one of those huge old oak trees where the broken branches have about 80 rings. Well, if you ever see one, sit at the bottom of it with your back against that part of the trunk leading directly to the main root; close your eyes and breathe deeply. Then just sit and listen...

Long before the woods, lakes and swamps became golf courses, shopping malls, and condominiums, but long after turtles got their shells, a turtle sat under a tall oak tree on the edge of a swamp. Every day around sunrise, this turtle would walk out of the swamp, make his way up the hill, sit under this tree in silence and look off into the distance. As animals who didn't know the turtle would pass by, they would often think he was in a trance. The truth of the matter was that in spite of the little pair of pincer glasses that sat on his face, this turtle couldn't see a thing – at least, not with his eyes.

Yes, he was a blind turtle that the other animals simply called 'Blind Turtle' (animals weren't much for being clever about names back then). Although Blind Turtle couldn't see the physical world, he was a turtle of great vision and insight. Once a week, when the turtle sat under the tree, he would speak. He'd tell stories and share his visions with anyone who might have been around (and there was always some animal hanging around). Animals, being curious by nature, often did go and visit the turtle in his silence and when he spoke. On the days that he spoke, animals would ask him why he sat in silence for so long. He would simply smile and say that he was listening to what the world was saying.

Of course, the animals didn't always see Blind Turtle as wise. At first, most of them thought Blind Turtle to be crazy or a fool and would walk away shaking their heads, figuring that he had gotten old and was losing his sense of reality. As time went by and more and more of Blind Turtle's visions came to pass, many of the animals realized that his visions were legitimate. Those animals would sit and listen, trying to hear what he heard, but all they heard were the birds singing, the wind blowing, the water in the stream running, the various calls and songs of the other animals, or their footsteps as they passed by on the road near the tree.

There was a meetinghouse a little further down the road where many of the animals gathered to listen to the preacher. By this time, snakes had formed the Snake Circle (which was really more of a coil), and were still trying to hatch their plots to control the lakes, woods and swamps. The Snake Circle began organizing a council of overseers in an effort to keep order – teaching the proper and civilized ways of snakes. The snake assigned to oversee this area was a slimy, little water moccasin named Phineas. When he slithered into the community and laid claim to the meetinghouse, he wasted no time in starting with his preaching about the natural inferiority of turtles, lizards, and frogs. He taught that only those who served and obeyed snakes might make it to the hereafter and while animals might not be able to become snakes, they could aspire to be snake-like. All things valuable and beautiful on the earth rightfully belonged to the snakes, he would say. After all of this, many of the animals stopped going to the meetinghouse, preferring to sit under the oak tree with Blind Turtle.

Phineas began to notice how thin his congregation was becoming, especially when it was time to tally up the income from the collection plate. He soon learned that many of his congregation was now going to the oak tree to listen to Blind Turtle. It was one thing to lose members of the congregation because they didn't want to come to meeting; it was something else entirely to lose them to a turtle. What could a turtle, especially a blind turtle, offer to the animals?

One morning, Phineas decided to slither down to the oak tree and see for himself what could possibly be so special about Blind Turtle. He hid down near the creek – just to the west of the tree – where he could see and hear without being detected. He saw Blind Turtle come out of the swamp and sit under the tree. As time passed, animals began to gather under the tree and sit with Blind Turtle. After a while, Blind Turtle began to speak about a bunch of visions that he had seen during the week and things that he heard in the wind… it all sounded like rubbish to the snake.

Blind Turtle began to talk about a vision of a lizard from another community who would come and provide help for them in a time of need. He suddenly stopped speaking, turned towards the creek, and called out, "Hey! You down there; yes, you… the snake. Why not come up and join us? It'll be a lot more comfortable here in the grass, under the shade of the tree." Phineas tried to lie still and pretended to be a branch, hoping that the other animals wouldn't see him. "I know you're there, snake. The voices in the wind told me you were there. It's okay, you can join us." All of the animals turned and saw Phineas laying flat along the creek, trying to look like a branch… until he sneezed. One of the animals began to snicker, which made a few of the other animals giggle, causing more to laugh out loud. Pretty soon, all of them were looking at Phineas eavesdropping on Blind Turtle, pointing and laughing at the snake as he slithered away in humiliation.

Things really began to take a downward turn for Phineas after that day. He was a laughing stock to all of the Snake

Circle. Imagine, a snake sneaking to a turtle's meeting! Fewer and fewer animals came to the meetinghouse and Phineas discovered what an echo the building had. Meanwhile, more and more animals were going to sit with the turtle under the oak tree, waiting for him to share a few words with those who gathered. Finally, Phineas decided that he would pay a visit to Blind Turtle and see for himself what the animal's attraction to this turtle was. Phineas surmised that if this turtle really had any power, it was the manifest destiny of snakes to control it.

On a day when Blind Turtle was sitting under the oak tree by himself, Phineas approached and asked if he could join him. The turtle nodded his head and continued with his meditations. Phineas sat quietly observing Blind Turtle as he continued to stare off into the distance in silence. After sitting in silence for what seemed to be an eternity, Phineas finally asked, "What are you listening to?"

"The voices." Replied Blind Turtle.

"What voices?"

"The voices of those who went before and those yet to come."

"Where do you hear these voices?"

"All around us."

"I don't hear anything."

"The voices are on the wind. They whistle through the branches of the trees and the rustle of the grass. The voices are all around; just listen."

Phineas tried to sit and listen and all he could hear was a breeze in the branches and leaves of the oak tree. Then, just when he was ready to give up listening, he thought he heard some voices. He wasn't sure, but somewhere in the whistle of the breeze in the tree, he heard them talking! He sat and listened for a while but was too excited to really pay attention. At last, he had the power of this old turtle. Phineas began visiting Blind Turtle rather regularly and would sit under the tree with him. One day, after a visit, he slithered back to his house where he wrote out a report to the Snake Circle about his discovery. Phineas' report caused quite a buzz (it sounded more like a hiss, actually) in the Snake Circle. As a result, he was soon regarded as an expert in dealing with the turtle population. The circle appointed a delegation of snakes to come and investigate Phineas' claim.

The delegation came out and decided to spend time at the tree with Blind Turtle. Most of them only heard the wind, but a few actually heard voices. Obviously, it was not a matter of the turtle having any powers (he was just a visually impaired turtle). It had to have something to do with the tree. They decided to examine the tree more closely, but it appeared to be just a plain, old oak tree. They took leaf and bark samples of the tree and ran all kinds of tests. Finally, the delegation issued the following report to the rest of the Snake Circle:

> After careful investigation and reviewing Phineas' claims about the oak tree and the turtle, some of us heard the voices that he spoke of. The turtle's ability to hear the voices can be explained rather simply: Turtles, being such simple and earthy creatures, can probably hear these voices because they have little else going on in their minds to distract them. We've come to the conclusion that the power that Phineas spoke of was in the tree itself.

Based on this report, the Snake Circle appointed all existing meetinghouses that were not made of oak to be torn down and replaced with oak structures. They also changed the procedure of the meeting: the snakes and congregation would gather in the oak meetinghouses and sit silently waiting for the voices to manifest. As quietly as they sat, all they heard was silence.

Meanwhile, Blind Turtle and the other animals continued to gather under the oak tree. Blind Turtle gave thanks to the ancestors for their wisdom and guidance, thanks to the trees, bushes, and grass for conveying this wisdom, and thanks to the crickets and small birds who sat in the tree and conversed on the days that Phineas and the members of the Snake Circle visited to oak tree.

To this day, you can still find snakes silently sitting among a meetinghouse congregation waiting to hear the voices.

~ SEVEN ~

BACKWOODS PEOPLE
Another Paradise Lost

Once upon a time,
It could have been yesterday;
It could have been today.
It could have been ten years ago;
It could have been ten years from now.
It really doesn't matter because,
IT'S ALL THE SAME AND
IT'S ALL GOOD, IN THE BACKWOODS!!!

Now, don't turn your nose up at the Backwoods*. It doesn't matter who you are or where you're from, if you go far enough back on your family tree (even as close as your parents or grandparents) you will find that you're from the Backwoods. Don't think for a second that being from Europe is going to save you either. I've read Sigmund Freud and *The Painted Bird*; I know Europeans have some deep, deep, deeeep backwoods. Backwoods people have a different philosophy on life. They adapt their lives to nature as opposed to making nature adapt to them. To Nowoods and Frontwoods people, this is considered "uncivilized". I can't really understand how people in the Nowoods don't even speak to each other and will even look away if somebody is in trouble, feel that they have the right to say who is "civil-" anything.

There is also very little in the way of race-prejudice in the Backwoods. You have dark and light-skinned people with kinky hair, straight hair, red hair, blonde hair, gray hair, white hair, no hair, brown eyes, hazel eyes, blue eyes, green eyes and gray eyes. Now, in most parts, this alone would be grounds for all kinds of problems – but not in the Backwoods. You see, in the Backwoods, almost everybody's related (regardless of what they look like). In the Backwoods, there's only one kind of prejudice – either you're from the Backwoods or you're not. Even still, if you're there long enough and they get to know you, that doesn't matter any longer because: IT'S ALL THE SAME AND IT'S ALL GOOD, IN THE BACKWOODS!!!

Where do Backwoods people come from? The answer is simple; they come from Backwoods parents, who came from Backwoods grandparents, who came from Backwoods great-grandparents... I guess I should start by telling you the Backwoods Creation story.

Yeah, that's right. Backwoods people even have their own creation story, and it goes a little something like this: A long time ago, there was this man and woman who were very rich and had everything they could ever want. The man decided to risk it all on some tip he'd gotten from a snake. The fool bet it all and lost it all. The couple fell on hard times and left their opulent lifestyle for a simple life in a shack. The shack was in a valley, down in between two mountains. Now, you know how people can get when they live in a shack, in a valley, in between two mountains; they begin to think that they are the only two people on the earth.

Years went by as they lived their life in this valley, farming, raising livestock and fishing in the stream. During these years, the couple had two sons, who grew up and helped their parents on the farm. Pretty soon, these two boys became teenagers and their hormones began to kick in. Well, you know how two teenage Backwoods boys can get when their hormones kick in. They began to argue and fight until one of them killed the other. Their father, being a typical Backwoods kind of man, attributed his son's outburst to the need for female companionship. How do you find a companion for somebody when there are only three of you in the world? You do the obvious thing; you venture up over one of the mountains and down to the riverbank where there's a camp with a whole bunch of women. The father went there, found a woman and brought her back for his son. When the father crossed back over the mountain and down into the valley with his daughter-in-law, he went to his son and said, "Here you go, Son. Here's woman of your own. Now, you can leave mine alone." Remember, when you are the only four people in the world, incest won't be illegal for another thirteen generations. Until then, IT'S ALL THE SAME AND IT'S ALL GOOD, IN THE BACKWOODS!!!

This brings us to the present, or near past or future. It doesn't really matter 'cause that's life in the Backwoods. In this Backwoods town, there is a Backwoods town center. Most folks who are not from the Backwoods end up driving through it while looking for civilization. If you're not from the Backwoods, folks just love to give you wrong directions, "The lake? Oh, yeah, that's about three miles before you come to Main Street," or something like that. In this Backwoods center there's a town hall, a library (yes, Backwoods folks read all kinds of books) and a tiny general store. On the wall next to the store's entrance, hung a "NO LOITERING" sign. Under the sign sat a whole bunch of folks from town, mostly very young and very old men. Sitting among these folks was the store's shopkeeper who was laughing, talking and telling stories with the rest of them. Now, if you're not from the Backwoods, you would probably think that this was loitering. But it's only loitering if they don't know you; otherwise it's socializing.

The shopkeeper is a kindly man, but is also a hard-core businessman. He watches every penny that comes into and goes out of the store. After all, if word got out that anyone had cheated him, his business would go down the tubes. One time, one of the local bad-asses decided that he was going to challenge the shopkeeper. The Backwoods bad-ass came in, made his selection, and came to the counter, saying "I ain't got the money right now, so I guess you'll hafta bill me." The shopkeeper quietly pointed to the sign on the wall behind him that read, "IN GOD WE TRUST. EVERYBODY ELSE PAYS CASH!" So the bad-ass told him that he was gonna take the stuff and that would be that. As he walked out of the store the shopkeeper came out behind him, tapped him on the shoulder, and punched the Backwoods bad-ass in the face. Then he started to beat the bad-ass' ass right there in the store's small parking lot. When he was done, he collected his goods and told the bad-ass, "No hard feelings!" – and you know what? There weren't any, 'cause IT'S ALL THE SAME AND IT'S ALL GOOD, IN THE BACKWOODS!!!

Another time, in this little store, a child wanted to buy some Backwoods Beef Jerky but was three cents short. The Shopkeeper told him that he couldn't sell it to him unless he came up with the three cents. The child began to look through his pants pockets for the change, but did it in that slow Backwoods way. A line began to form behind the child and nobody wanted to rush him 'cause that's the way folks are in the Backwoods. The line began to flow out of the store and down the street. Finally, one of the folks on line got a great idea. He reached into his pocket, pulled out three cents and gave it to the child; everybody was happy. Now this might have occurred to most people as the thing to do an hour earlier, but not around here, 'cause, IT'S ALL THE SAME AND IT'S ALL GOOD, IN THE BACKWOODS!!!

Down the street from the Backwoods store is a Backwoods bar. In the Backwoods bar you'll find Backwoods people sitting in the Backwoods tables and chairs and on the Backwoods bar stools having glass, after glass, after glass of Backwoods distilled spirits. As in any bar, the air is lively with all types of discussions – some of a base nature and some rather philosophical. Some discussions were feeble attempts at seduction and some were sincere vows of undying love.

If you know how any debate can go, you'll know that they can get heated. You may also know that if you add glass, after glass, after glass of distilled spirits to heat – you get combustion. You add Backwoods distilled spirits to a couple of Backwoods fools and you know that verbal communication comes to an end. Debates can turn into arguments; arguments can turn into fights; and.... I forgot to mention, Backwoods people love themselves some guns. So of course, this Backwoods fight becomes a Backwoods shoot-out such that the other Backwoods people in the Backwoods bar, run out of the bar through the doors and the windows. If you're not from the Backwoods, your assumption would be that they were trying to get their Backwoods asses out of there. NOPE! They ran out of the Backwoods bar to their Backwoods vehicles (mostly pick-up trucks and station wagons), grab their guns and run back into the Backwoods bar to join in on the shoot out. It doesn't really matter which side they join because IT'S ALL THE SAME AND IT'S ALL GOOD, IN THE BACKWOODS!!!

Now, I guess I should give you a glimpse into Backwoods domestic life. I would have to admit that I have a favorite Backwoods couple. Now I could tell you the story about how they used to court, she told him she never wanted to see him again, and he started seeing another woman. I could tell you about how his former-fiancée/now-wife heard about it and took a Backwoods gun and shot up every window in his house; but I'm not. I'm not even going to tell you how this led to his asking for her hand in marriage. I think we should move ahead several years and a few children later. The Backwoods wife was a Backwoods housewife. As the weather got colder, mice began to move into their Backwoods house. The mice took up residence in the Backwoods cabinets and shelves of the wife's' Backwoods kitchen and she told her husband about the problem. He'd said that he'd get to it in a couple of days. Well, you know how it gets. A couple of days turned into a couple of months and the husband didn't get around to it. The wife had enough and took her Backwoods children, packed some Backwoods belongings, got in her Backwoods family vehicle (a woodie station wagon) and went to stay with her mother who lived in the Back-Back-Backwoods. When the husband came home, he found his family gone.

He knew that his wife had been patient with him – really patient – 'cause Backwoods men are really honest that way. He knew that if he wanted her to come back, he was going to have to do something about the mice. Hunting season was coming up soon and he new that a lot of the guys would be around for a while, getting their guns ready and so forth. He was always able to think better after a few days of hunting, so he decided to go hunting with the guys on the next day. He got on the phone and invited a bunch of his friends over to stay the night in order to leave really early in the morning. He went to the Backwoods liquor store and bought several bottles of distilled spirits before coming home and making a big pot of Backwoods stew. Most Backwoods men are very good cooks, particularly since they're used to being left by their wives often.

That night, the guys sat around cleaning their guns, eating the stew, drinking and laughing. Everybody told him that the stew tasted like "[expletive]", which was a Backwoods male way of saying that it was exceptionally good. His response was "[expletive]", which was a Backwoods male way of saying "thanks". As the night wore on, the stew pot and the bottles of Backwoods distilled spirits grew emptier with each passing minute. Suddenly, a mouse appeared on the kitchen counter. The Backwoods husband saw the mouse, reached for his gun and shot at it. The mouse and a large chunk of the wall behind it was now gone. As the guys sat in the kitchen and laughed over a few glasses of distilled spirits, some other mice appeared and two more guys joined him in shooting at them.

Pretty soon, the whole group of them began shooting at the mice and the cabinets. The gunshots made big holes in the cabinets, counters and walls of the kitchen. It also punctured holes in the Backwoods canned goods and bottles that sat on the shelves and shattered the Backwoods china in the other cabinet. The mice who survived decided that it might be better to face the winter as field mice and quickly left the house through a small hole in the siding (which the husband said he'd fix a year ago).

The next morning, the Backwoods husband went out hunting with his partners. He figured that now that he'd gotten rid of his wife's' problem and deserved a little trip into the Back-Back-Back-Back-Backwoods. Two evenings later he called his wife and told her that the problem had been fixed and begged her to come home. She was quite happy to hear this, packed up her Backwoods kids, their Backwoods belongings and headed back to the Backwoods in her Backwoods vehicle (a *Woodie* station wagon). When the Backwoods wife got home and saw her kitchen, she just stood there and stared. She stared at the bullet riddled cupboards and cabinets. She looked at the syrup and juices from her Backwoods canned goods dripping out through the bullet holes. She gazed at the blasted boxes of Backwoods cornflakes, scattered all over the shelves, and the splinters of her Backwoods china. Her husband sat at the table, trying to get over his Backwoods hangover from the post hunting Backwoods cocktail party. The Backwoods wife looked at her kitchen, then to her husband. Slowly, she made her way across what was left of her kitchen and stood next to her husband, looking down at the back of his head. She picked up a frying pan (which had been dented by some ricocheted bullets), leaned over, and kissed her husband on the cheek. "Thank you, baby!" she exclaimed before making her way to the Backwoods stove to make a Backwoods breakfast for the family.

Later that day, the Backwoods husband went to the lumber yard and bought all new lumber and counter tops for the kitchen. The next day, his friends came over and the wife had herself a new kitchen. Now, to you, this might seem like a strange way to remodel, but remember, IT'S ALL THE SAME AND IT'S ALL GOOD, IN THE BACKWOODS!!!

Now, knowing that most folks who ain't from the Backwoods live in a state of denial, I realize that you probably don't recognize yourself in any of these scenarios. You probably even think that the Backwoods are all guns and illogical behavior. The fact of the matter is that these situations are exceptions to the rule, that's why they're stories. Who remembers the every day events; and who would be dumb enough to think that these stories were the norm anywhere? In the Backwoods, there is a lot of love and community. When it snows, Backwoods guys mount plows on their Backwoods vehicles (mostly pick-up trucks) and plow out the yards of the elderly folks and single mothers in town. In the fall, young folks rake the leaves out of their elder's yards.

Nobody ever goes hungry in the Backwoods because if you are going through hard times, there's always somebody there to lend you a hand. Children are raised to respect their elders in the Backwoods and almost everybody knows how to read. Sure, they drink Backwoods distilled spirits, but there is also a bar or liquor store on almost every corner in the Nowoods. Backwoods people hunt, but they hunt for food and fur – not for sport. People keep their doors unlocked in the Backwoods because they don't steal from each other and don't need to. When folks see empty forests in the Backwoods, they appreciate them for their beauty; they don't visualize a shopping mall – there's one twenty miles away and that's close enough.

If the Nowoods and the Frontwoods are civilization, then they can keep it. For me, IT'S ALL THE SAME AND IT'S ALL GOOD, IN THE BACKWOODS!!!

*Backwoods is capitalized because it is an ethno-cultural identity, like African, Native American, Latino, European, etc.

All of the cedar trees began to look the same and almost seemed as if they would close in on him.

~ Eight ~

A Lizard Appeared

Back in the days after snakes built meetinghouses out of oak, but before Rooster woke the sun; a lizard lived in a southern swamp community where the cedars grew tall and thick. One day while taking a walk, he got lost in the forest. All of the cedar trees began to look the same and almost seemed as if they would close in on him. A wind whistled through the trees and the voices told him to go to a place where the cedar trees grew in the swamp, the scrub pines grew plentifully, and the oak trees sprawled – a place where the voice of a Blind Turtle could be heard in the shade of an oak tree. Then the trees parted, the sun shined and the path reappeared. As one who paid attention to messages such as these, Fire Lizard soon set out from his own community towards the land of the swamps and scrub pines.

Fire Lizard was a very charming and well-spoken creature, as well as, a bit of an upstart. Some of the animals in his own community found him a little difficult to deal with because he was so outspoken; therefore, his departure was met with mixed feelings by the animals in the cedar lands. Fire Lizard would always take a stand when the snakes would impose upon the cedar community. Most of the animals in the tall cedars tried to not have any problems with the snakes, so they would often look the other way and let things be when the snakes tried to throw their weight around. It was the opinion of some of the animals that Fire Lizard's militant ways had caused the snakes to become so oppressive, believing that the snakes wouldn't bother them so much if it wasn't for Fire Lizard and his "trouble making."

One bright day, Fire Lizard set out to travel away from his home among the tall cedars towards the swamp community. It was a good thing that he left, too. Unbeknownst to Fire Lizard; there was a plot brewing among some members of his community to take him down a notch or two by selling him into indentured servitude to the snakes. His arrival in the swamp community was of little surprise to anybody, as Blind Turtle had predicted his appearance a while back. Even the animals who weren't at the oak tree on the day of Blind Turtle's revelation knew about Fire Lizard. How couldn't they? Stuff-talking Chipmunk went about telling everybody. Stuff-talking Chipmunk was quite a character. Most of the animals found him both annoying and engaging all at the same time. Because chipmunks travel on the ground and in the trees, they see things from a lot of different perspectives and points of view. They also move very quickly, so they see a lot of things in a short amount of time.

These attributes caused Stuff-talking Chipmunk to believe that he was an authority everything. He always had something to say, and you could usually hear him long before you saw him coming. "If Blind Turtle had a vision that a lizard was coming, then there has to be something to it...", said Stuff-talking Chipmunk, "so, we'd better be ready for him when he arrives. You know Blind Turtle doesn't just say stuff for no reason. If he saw a lizard coming, then there's a reason..." Stuff-talking Chipmunk went on and on while helping the other animals to prepare a place for the lizard to live when he arrived. Knowing that the lizard was coming from the land of the tall cedars, they made a home for him in the roots of one of the larger cedar trees in the middle of the swamp.

Since his journey required him to travel through areas that were densely settled by snakes, Fire Lizard decided to use the branches of the scrub pine trees for his passage – most of the snakes couldn't get up that high to bother him. However, all of the jumping, climbing and scrabbling left the lizard kind of pooped. It was a little before sunrise when Fire Lizard arrived in the land of the swamps. Owl, who was on her way home with some breakfast for her family, spotted Fire Lizard, greeted him, and showed him to his new home in the swamp. Fire Lizard thanked Owl, entered his new home, unpacked and settled in. He decided that he'd take a nap for about an hour before going about introducing himself to his new neighbors. He curled up on his bed and closed his eyes.

A little after noon, a paw banging on the front door awakened Fire Lizard. He yawned, stretched, and went to answer the door, only to be greeted by Stuff-talking Chipmunk. "Well, hey there sleepy-head! Rise and shine. What where you doing – partying too hard last night? Time to get up and get out; animals are waiting to meet you!" Fire Lizard rubbed his eyes as this demented chipmunk rambled on and on, "… Blind Turtle said you were coming. Some folks doubted him, but I can tell you that I believed him. I always did listen to that wise old turtle; more animals should. I always say, and always have said… Mark my words and listen to me, I always know what I'm talking about…" Fire Lizard went to his cupboard to make a pot of tea as the chipmunk followed him continuing, "Sorry – allow me to introduce myself. My name is Chipmunk… Stuff-talking Chipmunk. I know; that's an odd-sounding name, isn't it? Well it's my name and I live at the edge of the swamp, but I don't have problems coming in the swamp, nope, no problems at all. Most chipmunks…" Fire Lizard calmly poured two cups of tea, setting one in front of the chipmunk who had finally settled into a seat at the kitchen table. He also served some acorn biscuits figuring that if he enticed the chipmunk into eating and drinking, he might stop talking for a few seconds.

As Stuff-talking Chipmunk slowed down to enjoy his snack, Fire Lizard took the opportunity to ask Chipmunk direct questions about the community. He wanted to know about issues and events in the community, how to find Blind Turtle, how the snakes in the community behaved, how the animals in the swamp protect themselves from the snakes, and so on. Between munching on the acorn biscuits and sipping his tea, Stuff-talking Chipmunk answered all of Fire Lizard's questions. Stuff-talking Chipmunk was on his way to have one of his weekly sessions with Blind Turtle and invited Fire Lizard to come along. As they made their way through the swamp, Stuff-talking Chipmunk stopped to talk stuff to just about every animal they met – introducing Fire Lizard to them as the lizard that Blind Turtle predicted to appear. "See? Blind Turtle said he was coming and I told you, too. Now, see? Here he is, just like we said. You need to learn to listen to us..." Before the animals could have a chance to respond or introduce themselves to Fire Lizard, Stuff-talking Chipmunk would whisk him away. "Come on. We're running late. We gotta go see Blind Turtle..." he would say.

When they reached the oak tree, they found Blind Turtle sitting beneath it as usual, with a smile on his face. Before Stuff-talking Chipmunk could begin his litany, Blind Turtle said to Fire Lizard, "Welcome, my friend. It's good to finally meet you. Have a seat and make yourself comfortable." The chipmunk and the lizard joined the turtle under the tree. Surprisingly, Chipmunk actually allowed the other two animals to speak to each other, liberally interjecting comments and commentary. When it was time for the chipmunk and lizard to leave, Blind Turtle invited Fire Lizard to return whenever he'd like... alone.

Fire Lizard took to visiting and sitting with the turtle several times a week. Fire Lizard was sure to make these visits without the chipmunk; Blind Turtle had set up a designated time that Stuff-talking Chipmunk could come and visit him under the oak tree. Without a set schedule, chipmunk would come see him all of the time – talking on and on about all kinds of things. Not only was Blind Turtle not particularly one for swamp gossip, but also the chipmunk's chatter interrupted his meditation time. Fire Lizard suggested that the turtle serve acorn biscuits to Stuff-talking chipmunk as a way to slow him down. During their conversations, Blind Turtle and Fire Lizard would discuss all kinds of things, including the time, years ago, when Blind Turtle visited the land of the tall cedars.

Fire Lizard couldn't help but notice the rapid way with-which oak, poplar, elm, and chestnut trees seemed to be disappearing from the edge of the swamp. He brought this up during a visit with Blind Turtle who explained that the snakes had come up with a rule that made the territory common property that snakes could take from whenever they pleased. They would enter the "common property" of the swamp region and get wood for their homes, fires and other needs. This rule was especially unfair because the snakes had made their land essentially untouchable. They ruled that Snake land belonged to the snakes and nothing could be removed from it without the express permission of a snake. The penalty for breaking this rule was indentured servitude (to the snakes, of course) for a period of seven years. Blind Turtle explained that his oak tree would soon be up for grabs unless the animals were able to do something; however, most of them were afraid of the snakes.

Fire Lizard was greatly disturbed by what he'd heard from the turtle. Had these snakes no respect? Blind Turtle and his oak tree were considered legendary throughout all of the animal communities and now they were going to cut the oak tree down like it was nothing. Something had to be done! Fire Lizard stayed up most of the night thinking, plotting, and making notes. The next day, Stuff-talking Chipmunk came by for his usual visit. Fire Lizard had a pot of tea and a heaping plate of acorn biscuits ready for their discussions about politics, community issues, and visions for the future. This day, Fire Lizard had an idea that involved the chattering chipmunk. As Fire Lizard served him tea and acorn biscuits, he shared his notes – implying that they were both confidential and very important. For the first time since they'd met, Stuff-talking Chipmunk listened more then he spoke.

The next day, Fire Lizard purposely stayed out of the sight of most of the animals, including Stuff-talking Chipmunk. He did, however, make his visit to Blind Turtle for their regular dialogue. The day after that, Fire Lizard got up to take his morning walk and decided to go to the middle of the swamp. He found a nice perch on a felled tree and sat there as the rays of the sun cut through the branches of the trees. At exactly noon, Fire Lizard started to recite a poem in a very animated fashion and the animals of the swamp slowly started to gather around him to listen. You see, the day before, Stuff-talking Chipmunk had gone around telling all of the animals about his 'conversation' with Fire Lizard and all of the ideas and concepts that Fire Lizard shared with the chipmunk and the curious animals wanted to hear some of it for themselves – Fire Lizard's plan had worked!

There was a certain degree of audience participation involved in this recitation and the audience became quite lively in responding to the words of Fire Lizard's poem. Among the crowd was the chipmunk, hyping the crowd as they listened to the lizard, "Yeah, lizard! Tell it like it is reptile! Yeah! Speak your truth!" When Fire Lizard was done, he disappeared into the swamp. The animals had never heard anything like this before and the poem became the main topic of discussion among those who dwelled in the swamp. Stuff-talking Chipmunk went around visiting the animals that weren't there when Fire Lizard recited his poem saying, "Wow! You missed it! It was incredible! This is what you *really* need to hear…" The next day, when Fire Lizard went to the middle of the swamp he found a crowd of animals already waiting for him. This time, when he recited his poems there was an even bigger crowd. This went on for a couple of weeks.

One day, Blind Turtle sat at his oak tree and was paid a visit by a group of snakes that had come to inform him that they were there to cut down the tree. It was a big, old tree that could be turned into lots and lots of lumber. They said that allowing it to remain a tree for animals to sit under was a waste of good wood. Blind Turtle's heart sank as the snakes told him that he had three minutes to vacate the premises. Just as Blind Turtle was about rise, he felt a paw on his shoulder (well, on where his shoulder would be). It was Stuff-talking Chipmunk, "He doesn't have to go anywhere! In fact, you have three minutes to clear out of here yourselves." the chipmunk declared.

"What?!?" hissed the fore-snake.

"Yeah! That's right! That's what I said! You heard me!" continued Stuff-talking Chipmunk.

"How dare you! Do you know who you're talking to?"

"Some snake as far as I can see. What's that supposed to mean to me?"

The snakes started to move in on Stuff-talking Chipmunk and Blind Turtle until a voice said, "I suggest you snakes look behind you." It was Fire Lizard with a small army of swamp animals. They had the oak tree and the snakes surrounded and looked very ready for a confrontation. The snakes knew they were in trouble and watched in helpless anger as the animals unpacked the snakes' wagon full of lumber, took away their weapons, and sent them back to the snake community empty-handed and humiliated. They quickly went to the Snake Circle and required an injunction against the swamp community and an arrest warrant for the Blind Turtle, Fire Lizard, and Stuff-talking Chipmunk. They were reluctantly denied the injunction and the warrants because, by their own laws, Blind Turtle was he rightful owner of the tree by squatter's rights and the chipmunk had the right to defend him. The lizard, on the other hand, was an outside agitator and did not have the right to do what he did – including instigating the removal the lumber from the snake's cart. Almost immediately, a militia of snakes marched… I mean slithered into the swamp territory expecting to shake down the animals in an effort to locate Fire Lizard and reinstate their authority. When they came over the hill into the swamp they did not expect to be greeted by a militia of swamp animals poised to defend themselves.

During the standoff, Fire Lizard had snuck out of the community headed toward points unknown. He knew that falling into the hands of the snakes would be his ultimate demise. Some say that he went back to his own community; others say he went elsewhere, sparking more uprisings and revolts against snakes.

Much to the surprise of most of the animals, Stuff-talking Chipmunk emerged as a vital and effective organizer of the swamp community. In fact, to this day you can still hear the chatter of chipmunks in the swamp, warning other animals about an approaching snake.

Blind Turtle continued to sit under the oak tree for many years; listening to the voices of the ancestors on the wind until the day he joined them. However you look at it, all you need to spark an uprising is a little fire and a stuff-talker.

~ Nine ~

Rooster & Fox

There was a house in the animal land... the house of Rooster, where the sun rose. It might not be much to look at these days, but it wasn't always the coop that it is now. You see, long, long after Rooster had given up the ministry to become the sun's alarm clock, and long before blind turtles preached under oak trees, Rooster was given another job where he began to dabble in politics. Dabble was all that he could do because at that time, politics didn't pay a whole lot of money – at least not above board. How he got into politics was an accident and it went a little like this:

After Rooster began singing every morning to wake up the sun, he began to see this post as being very important and worthy of the grandness of a rooster. He used to strut around proudly with his chest stuck out. Most of the other animals found this quite amusing, as they knew he didn't wake the sun at all. Even so, his arrogance really began to get to them after a while. Some of the animals began to complain to Turtle who felt that if it gave him such a sense of satisfaction to believe that he was waking the sun, let him think what he was.

One weekend, the animal council got together to nominate and select the right animals to fulfill the various leadership roles within the community. The whole council decided to give Rooster the highest profile, yet least influential appointment of them all.

"Ambassador to what?" Rooster asked of the small group of animals standing at his door to officially offer him the appointment.

"Uh... Ambassador to the neighboring communities," replied Miss Doe (A Deer. A Female Deer), leader of the *Animal Appointment Delegation.*

In these days, the animal territory was vast and nobody was living in the outlands, so the need for Rooster to do anything was virtually non-existent.

Rooster was, indeed, a clever bird. He understood the dynamics of leadership and the importance of delegating authority and function. How else could an animal have 21 wives living together in the same house and none of them get upset about it? Yes, in a room full of chickens, he was the king; but he had problems mixing with the other animals. He was just not much of a peo... uh, "animal of the animals." Being a clever animal, Rooster realized that he would need to enlist the aid of an animal that was as regal and as clever as he was. He'd also need someone that had more of a *common touch* to walk among the animals. The perfect choice for the job was his best friend, Fox. Rooster went to the animal council and requested that Fox be named his Deputy Ambassador.

Rooster and Fox set up their offices and waited for an opportunity to carry out their duties, but no such opportunity came. Pretty soon, their office became more of place for Rooster and Fox to show off to the animals that they wanted to impress and a hang out for their friends to play cards and drink wild berry juice – a concoction made by Mr. Raccoon in wooden barrels. Sometimes, Rooster would end up consuming so much juice that he could be found asleep in the tall grass next to his office. Sometimes, some of the animals would amuse themselves by shouting for Rooster to wake up, saying that he was being summoned to duty on some diplomatic move. Rooster would jump up, dust himself off and try to straighten up and look dignified as the animals walked off laughing.

A Mixed Medicine Bag

One day, although it really happened over a period of time, people began appearing in the outlands. They ripped down trees, built houses, and fired guns. This distressed the animals greatly. Rooster, whose diplomatic territory was the outlands, now had a position of great importance to the animal community. This also distressed many of the animals greatly, as five chickens that had been out for a walk had already disappeared. Some of the council members got together in small meetings trying to find a technicality by which to remove Rooster from his position, but none existed. Even if they'd found one, none of the other animals wanted the job. Who'd want to be a diplomatic representative to a community that shoots at you every time they see you out taking a stroll or eating your lunch? So, like it or not, the animals were stuck with Rooster as their diplomatic representative to the people.

Fox suggested that the best way to deal with people was to be prepared to answer questions and Rooster agreed. They sat and brainstormed, deciding how the animal land would be explained in human terms. Most birds and owls got trees and were generally allowed squatter's rights wherever they landed; seagulls got waterfront property and dump areas; snakes, turtles, frogs, and lizards got the swamps, marshes, and bogs; raccoons, squirrels, chipmunks, mice, deer, foxes, and so forth got the inlands. Back in those days, farmland was planted by crows and maintained by the cows and horses. The easily domesticated animals like horses, pigs, cows, dogs, ducks, geese, and lambs were allowed rights to it. Rooster and Fox also outlined the common lands, next to the lake, that were owned by all of the animals. They figured that, at some time or another, most of the animals would want to fish, swim or drink fresh water. The last point that they took on was that there were predators among the animals. They knew that a lot of the people were hunters which, given the predators, was reasonable. Rooster and Fox stipulated; however, that that the hunters needed to give the animals a sporting chance. With that, they designed a four-point platform – a declaration, of sorts, to present to the people. Rooster had hired some young chicken to be his secretary. She typed up the animal land description and Declaration:

1. **No person can hunt animals within the territory of the animal community.**
2. **No person can take away an animal's land.**
3. **No person can interfere with Animal Council activities or have the right to vote.**
4. **Trade may be carried out between animals and people only under conditions that were safe for all involved.**

Rooster and Fox used a messenger (some pigeon) to deliver their letter of introduction and request for a meeting to the people. A couple of days later, the messenger returned with a note from the people. They wanted to meet with Rooster in three days. "What about me?" asked Fox, clearly disappointed by being slighted and not included in the invite. "Well, we need to have somebody to run the office while I'm out. As Deputy Ambassador, you have to take over when I'm not available." This did make Fox feel a better, but only a little.

The night before Rooster's trip to the outlands, he couldn't sleep a wink. When he finally dozed off, he almost missed sunrise. This was his big chance to do something for his community and to show the other animals what a smart and capable bird he was – he didn't want to mess this up. This time, he was going to fight for what was right for the animals and not just himself. As he crossed the border into the outlands, he marveled at how much they had built up their town. What used to be woods and meadows were now houses, stores, libraries, and town buildings. He made his way through town until he got to their town hall and went into his meeting. Rooster mused about how great it might be to have these things in the animal community.

The young secretary to the Mayor of the People greeted rooster. She smiled and asked him to have a seat. Rooster looked around at the waiting room, taking in the fact that the secretary's office was much bigger and fancier than his own back in the animal community. After several minutes, which felt like several hours, Rooster was finally called into the mayor's office. Mayor of the People sat at a big desk in a big, comfortable-looking chair. His office was the fanciest room in the entire building. The walls were trimmed with gold and the fireplace had a marble mantle. The mayor sat at his desk with a big grin on his face. He warmly greeted Rooster and invited him to sit in a nice, big, armchair near the fireplace. Mayor of the People offered Rooster a drink, which he accepted, and a cigar. Rooster found the drink to be a little strong, but very enjoyable. It was something called "scotch and soda".

Rooster remembered why he'd come and was ready to launch into his position, while puffing on his cigar and sipping his drink, when the mayor started saying how happy he was that such a smart and civilized animal was chosen to be the Ambassador for the animal community. "I know you to be a bird of great intelligence, leadership, and integrity. You are a bird of vision, who understands that times change." said the mayor. He continued, "I see big things on the horizon for animals and people alike. Can I freshen your drink?"

"Thank you."

The meeting lasted a long time and Rooster gave the mayor a copy of the Declaration. As Rooster began to feel light and tingly from the drink, the mayor fixed him another one. He could tell that it had a little more scotch in it this time. The mayor glanced at the Declaration and said, "I'm sure this won't be an issue." The mayor went on to offer Rooster supplies and resources for the animal community. "I'm here to help you all to help yourselves." explained the mayor.

Trying not to sound too anxious, Rooster said that he would discuss the mayor's kind offer with the Animal council and get back to him. Rooster went home from the meeting feeling very proud of himself, carrying a box of cigars under his wing. It was a little *"gift"* from Mayor of the People. In all of his excitement, he'd completely forgotten to ask about the five missing chickens. In the grander scheme of diplomatic relations, he decided to let it go. When Rooster gave his report to the council, he made it sound as if he had intimidated the mayor into offering help to the animals. Of course, the animals took this spin with a grain of salt, but were glad to hear that the mayor seemed to be a reasonable individual. Rooster made many visits to the outlands after that, each time coming home with a report about how nice and cordial everybody was.

The council decided that they needed to check it out for themselves and appointed a delegation of animals to visit the town. Rooster also noticed that his friend, Fox, was feeling a bit left out. He decided that he'd send Fox with the delegation as his representative. About a week later, Fox, Cow, Duck, Horse, Doe (A deer, a female…), and Pig were sent into the outlands to meet with Mayor of the People and the other officials. The people welcomed the animals and threw a great, big party in their honor (with lots of food). As Fox was the official Ambassador of the delegation, he was called into a special meeting while the other animals were given a tour of the people town. The animals were so awe-struck because of the things they were seeing that they also forgot to ask about the five chickens that were still missing.

At diplomatic meetings in the outlands, delicious meals were served. On the first night, a delicious meat was served with rice and vegetables. Fox had never tasted such delicacy. In the morning, Fox was served sumptuous breakfast of puffy, cloud-looking, yellow things and two strips of meat. He had two helpings. Meanwhile, the news of the day was the disappearance of Pig. That evening, the people held an affair called a 'picnic' where the same kind of meat as the night before was served fried with potato salad and watermelon on the side. Strange things were happening; the next morning over breakfast the news of Cow being felt up in the dark by some weirdo, began to circulate. As Fox listened, he began to eat his meal. Afterwards, Fox had a drink called 'coffee' (which was quite nice) with a thick, white fluid added. Later he tried a delicious, broiled meat called 'barbecue' followed by a dessert called 'ice cream'.

That evening, only Fox and Doe returned to the animal lands. Doe was told by the people to be sure and return when she was bigger, and to bring friends. When they reached the animal community, Fox told Rooster about the other animals. Rooster promptly sent a message to Mayor of the People inquiring about the rest of the delegation that never made it home.

Rooster noted a change in his friend's personality. Fox started coming by Rooster's house more after work and hanging out late at night, talking. Fox seemed sort of nervous and distracted, which was not at all like him. Rooster's concern for his friend turned to complete horror when he came into the office one morning, only to find Fox sitting at his desk eating the secretary... a young chicken. The messenger returned with a note from Mayor of the People, on grease stained paper, wrapped around a cigar. It appeared that

Cow, Duck and Horse were taken into indentured servitude to pay of the expenses of housing and entertaining the delegation. Nobody seemed to know what happened to pig. The mayor continued to offer whatever assistance was required.

Meanwhile, Rooster was very troubled by his best friend's strange new behavior (and taste for chicken). They ran through five secretaries in two weeks until Rooster hired Ms. Lizard. He would come home from work and find Fox and some of his kind, hanging around outside of his house staring at the chickens through the window. Rooster sought a restraining order from the Animal Council, but Fox was within his rights under the predatory codes. In an act of desperation, Rooster turned to Mayor of the People for assistance. The mayor made Rooster a wonderful offer: a house would be built for Rooster and his entire family on the Mayor's own estate, and the house would be guaranteed Fox-proof. Rooster agreed whole-heartedly and let out a great sigh of relief.

When Rooster and his family arrived at the mayor's estate, they found Cow, Duck, and Horse grazing out in the meadow rather contentedly. He also found three of the five chickens that had been missing, living in the coop that he moved into with his family. Cow had even formed a kind of friendship with the weirdo who would visit her in the night; she also fell for some bull. The ducks actually liked the easy life of swimming in the pond and being fed ground corn by the mayor's wife.

However, while the other animals roamed free, Rooster and his family had to remain in a sort of 'protective custody' – locked in the coop. They would look out at the rest of the world through a mesh fence. Every so often, Fox and his kin will wander into the Town of the People and hang around outside of the chicken coop. They would normally try to find a hole in the fence or a loose board that would allow them to sneak in. Rooster, who was never afraid of Fox, himself, would often stand guard. Eventually, Mayor of the People and his dogs made a sport of chasing Fox and his kin, while riding Horse and his children. Rooster and Fox were never friends again and Rooster went back to his old job of waking the sun.

Rooster and Fox also outlined the common lands, next to the lake, that were owned by all of the animals. They figured that, at some time or another, most of the animals would want to fish, swim or drink fresh water.

~ Ten ~

A CHILD WAS BORN

In the northeastern region of Africa, there was a kingdom and in the kingdom, a village. About 400 years before this story took place, this particular village had been the birthplace of Faruq – the legendary king who brought knowledge, wisdom and understanding to the land, building libraries, schools and universities. Under the dynasty of Faruq, knowledge was considered as gold. However, 380 years after his rise to power, his dynasty came to an end. The village where he was born had changed from a solid and interconnected community to a small city, with a merchant class who controlled everything. You see, the long-standing organizational structure of village's government had disappeared. In the old days, there was an elder's council, a council of scholars, a matriarch's council and so forth who made the decisions about how things in the community would be run.

Although the old system was very effective and fair, it was completely replaced by a much more modern system of elected and appointed officials. The monarchs of the kingdom no longer concerned themselves with the legislative affairs of the land; their position was now mainly ceremonial. The merchant class made up about one-tenth of the village's population, but controlled most of the community's resources. Most of the village's population was not allowed to vote because they didn't own land and/or were deeply in debt to a wealthier citizen. Whereas the old system seemed to take the concerns and welfare of the people into account, the new system followed two simple rules when it came to things that affected the village:

1.) What would it cost the village?
2.) What benefit would it be to the village?

Of course, the third unspoken criterion was:

3.) What would it profit the officials and/or their friends?

Knowledge was no longer golden; in fact, most people who would have been considered prophets and teachers in Faruq's time were now dismissed as insane and often turned away to live in the streets. At one time, all people were treated and considered equal. The new system, however, recognized people's status and rights in the order of property owners, business owners, taxpayers, and then everybody else.

In this village, a child was born. This would not be considered an unusual event in any village; in fact, no one really cared. No one from the village gathered outside of the house, awaiting the child's birth. Particularly since this child was marked from before his birth as a point of shame for his family. His mother was a simple teenaged girl and the child's father had not been disclosed. Although there had been rumors as to who had fathered the child, the girl and her mother said nothing. In time, the child's mother disappeared, leaving him to be raised by his grandmother (who was still a young woman, herself, only in her Understanding Equality degree – 36 years). The child's grandmother had also given birth to a child at an early age. The father of her child was disclosed; however, he was a married man with children so he dismissed her. Society's standards being what they were, the woman was spurned and the man's actions were simply described as an *indiscretion*.

It was a long-standing custom that the others in the village aided the poor and sick of the village. Of course, the officials had formalized this custom. This formal law of supporting the poor and sick was a simple structure. The recipients of this support had to agree to enter indentured servitude to those who supported them, particularly males. In this case, the grandmother sought support for her grandchild with the understanding that he would enter servitude in his Power degree (5 years old), and remain until his Knowledge Freedom degree (14 years old). The village officials created this system as a solution to two problems:

1. The growing population of poor people in the village.
2. The low number of male children being born into the wealthier families in the community.

With fewer males, the merchants and landowners had fewer hands to help them with their work. For some reason, the poor were able to produce more children and therefore, had more males.

Although the grandmother hated to do this, she knew that she had to get money to clothe and feed the child for those first five years – children grew so very rapidly then. On the day that he reached his Power degree (5th year), he was collected and hauled off to his first charge. He came to work for a man who owned a farm. On the farm, the man raised animals to sell at the market. The boy's task was to clean the animal pens and prepare their feed – a combination of ground up grain and molasses. This was hard work for a grown man, let alone a small child, but he carried out his tasks. If he didn't, he was punished with a harsh beating and no food for that night. The child was given a corner in the barn with the animals for his living space that consisted of a palette to sleep on, a hook upon which to hang his clothing and a bowl for his meals. Once every moon (about a month), he was allowed to go home for a visit.

After the boy had been on the farm for about three years, the farmer's wife had a baby boy. According to the laws, the servant boy was to be sent to another sponsor's place to work. For the next several years the young man was sent from sponsor to sponsor where he was given very difficult tasks and treated very badly. The nicest name that anybody had for him was "Boy". Other titles generally referred to the fact that his parents were not married. Growing up, only two people showed the child any kindness: his grandmother and an old man who lived on the street, drank wine and talked endlessly about weird mathematical equations. He would talk about the sun, moon and stars, the distance of the earth from the sun and the position of the planets. The young boy would sneak out at night, visit his grandmother and bring the old man food on his way back to his sponsor's house. Using tattered old scrolls that the old man claimed to be several hundred years old, he taught the boy how to read. This continued until the boy reached his Knowledge Wisdom degree (about 12 years) and was discovered by his sponsor, who was coming home from a tavern. The sponsor punished the boy and told him, "If you listen to that foolish old man, you'll end up just like him!"

It was a custom in the village that when a male, any male, reached his Knowledge Freedom degree (about 14 years) he was to have his first rite of passage into manhood. The boy had just reached his Knowledge Understanding degree (about 13 years) and was looking forward to the end of this year. Not only would he be free to live with his grandmother again, but he could freely study with the old man. Maybe his grandmother would even let him bring the old man home to live with them. However, as the boy dreamed of his approaching freedom, the officials met to discuss a problem of finances for the village. There was not a lot of money in the village treasury and they were already seriously in debt. The answer to their problem was to sell some assets, but what? What could they sell that would not be considered a loss to the village? They decided to table the discussion for another meeting.

A few days later, a group of men on horseback rode into the town. They were a group of raiders who were looking for new recruits for their fold. So fierce were these men that the strongest and toughest of all men bowed to them as they passed through. They could, and if so desired would, take anything that they wanted from anybody. However, they would always ask first and even offer money, giving the person the opportunity to peacefully hand it over. The raiders said that they were willing to pay gold for any strong young men who could join their band. The officials took this as a sign from above; this would be the answer to their problems. They would sell the raiders all of the strong young indentured servants in the village and the gold would be enough to pay off most of the debts. Additionally, they would not have to go to the expense of giving these young men a Rite of Passage Ceremony! Without even a word, the young men were rounded up and sent off with the raiders, including the young boy. He was not even allowed to say goodbye to his grandmother. The raiders led their new recruits off into the west.

Five years had passed. Life in the village was pretty much the same except that there seemed to be more people, more businesses, and more folks living in the streets. One evening, as the sunset, the outline of a group of people could be seen way off into the distance. They were riding on horses. As the group got closer, it was clear that these were a group of raiders being lead by none other than the young boy, who was now a young man. He was a thick and muscular young man with arms the size of a big man's legs. The young man led his band of warriors into the town. As they rode in, the villagers took refuge in their homes and shops, peeking out from time to time to see what was going to happen. The only people on the streets were the poor and homeless, many of whom did not seem too concerned by the presence of these dangerous guests. They stopped in the town's square where they demanded to see the town's treasurer. The treasurer appeared and was commanded to turn over all of the gold in the treasury. He obeyed and the young man tossed the gold into the air, allowing all of the street people to gather it.

The young man raised his sword and pointed in the direction of the market place as he uttered something in a different language. The other raiders began riding through the town, burning and slashing the market place. As merchants came out of hiding to protect their stores, the raiders and their horses killed them. The young man stopped at the house of his first sponsor, released all of the animals and set fire to the house. He then went to each of the homes and businesses of his sponsors in the order that he had served them, and burned them to the ground – sending the sponsors and their families fleeing for their lives. Many of them were not fortunate; they were trampled in the melee. The young man went to the home of his grandmother and went in. Tears of joy and pride welled up in her eyes as she saw her grandson. He took her out of the house and placed her on his horse. He then found the old man who had been so good to him and placed him on his horse, as well. He ran into the temple, returning minutes later with a black box tucked under his arm, and led his band of raiders off as the village burned behind them. The raiders came to a high hill overlooking the village and the young man let his grandmother and the old man off of the horse. He kissed her goodbye, explaining that his lifestyle was not good for her, but that she would be safe there. He directed her toward another village, a few steps beyond, where she and the old man could establish new lives.

The young man and his band of raider warriors rode off, never looking back. The old man and the woman watched the raiders disappear into the rising sun. They then turned to see that their old village was now just a pile of ashes and rubble. In time, the winds and the rains would erase any trace of the village's existence. The old man raised his flask of wine, paused and said, "Well, I guess it does take a child to RAZE a village." Then he took a long, slow drink of the wine as he and the old woman made their way to the nearby village.

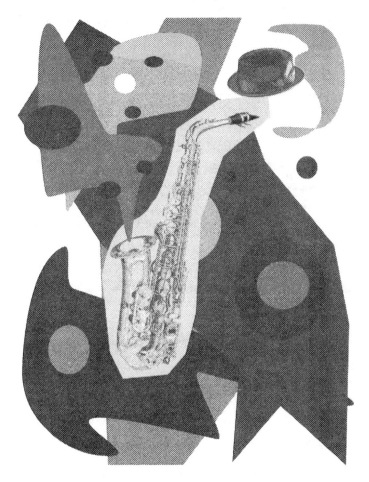

Clement lifted the sax to his lips, took a deep breath and began to play. The melody that flowed from the sax was unlike anything that he'd ever played before.

~ ELEVEN ~

THE DUET

There's a place in between being asleep and awake where our minds are locked into everything that has ever existed or ever will exist. We can see the unseen and feel the intangible. As we drift back into consciousness and our eyes open, the world around us is just a series of patterns of swirling lights, colors and sounds. This is the place where artists dwell, even when they're in the physical world.

Northeast Bronx, N.Y. Circa 1985

The sun hung in the cloudless sky – the way that it always does on a January morning – giving off a cold, orange glow. It was Saturday and the streets were slowly coming to life with millions of 9-5'ers staying in bed for extra hours, while their kids sat in front of televisions watching cartoons over bowls of cereal. Remains of cheap wine sitting in bottles on curbs and in alleys were evidence of winter night meetings that happen on some of the corners.

In all of this, the city held a certain beauty that could be felt and not seen. The randomness of the ten million inhabitants was like a heavily orchestrated piece of music with pulses, harmonies, melodies, themes, variations and tempos. The view through each apartment window was like changing the channels on a television with a strong satellite dish. Each room was similar, but had enough differences to make them separate worlds.

A row of three-story homes sat on a deserted, tree-lined street. The door to one of these homes opened, out of which stepped a youth of about seventeen years of age. He was dressed like an average teenager from the city – in boots, baggy jeans, and a winter jacket. On his head he wore a pork-pie hat. His hair was in a neat Afro, which stuck out from under the brim of the hat. Slung across his shoulder was a soft saxophone case, containing the brass sax that his uncle had given him years ago. The young man's name was Clement Pells.

Clement had grown up on this block. He knew everybody and everybody knew him. In his seventeen years, the whole area hadn't changed very much. Some people would move away and some people would move in but most of the folks who lived in these houses stayed right where they were because it was home. Most of the folks living in that neighborhood had come up from either the south or the West Indies, years before, in search of a new life. Owning a home, as most of the families on this block did, represented that dream. In the spring and summer months, folks would be working in their small yards and doing minor repair work to their houses.

Clement's father was from New Bedford, Massachusetts, and a descendant of Black and Wampanoag whalers. He went to Howard University and became a campus radical. However, a corporate headhunter came to campus and lured him to New York with a really good job offer at the phone company. Mr. Pells traded in his dashiki for a suit, tie, and life in a new place.

Clement glanced over at his buddy Yusef's house, but there was no evidence of anybody being awake yet. Yusef played piano and African drums, a skill he learned from his father. Yusef's father ran a local community arts center that a lot of the kids in the area went to. On warm days he would lead drum circles in the park and Yusef, Clement and another buddy Ian (who was now called "Atif") participated. At the end of the block was Atif's house. Atif played trap kit drums and was a D.J. As Clement got closer to Atif's house, he could hear the muffled sounds of a hip-hop beat coming from Atif's basement. Because it had been soundproofed, it was the only place that Atif could practice all night. For some reason, although he couldn't be heard in the rest of the house, the sound still bled out into the street through a basement window.

Clement went around to the back of the house and knocked on the basement door. Within a few seconds, the door swung open and a tired-looking Atif appeared. He had been up all night playing with his equipment. Clement stepped into the basement room. It had rugs on all of the walls and soundproof ceilings. Tapes and records contained within boxes and crates were on one side of the room and Atif's D.J. and recording equipment sat to the opposite side. Atif and Clement had grown up together and their mutual love of music gave them a strong bond. "What've you been up to?" asked Clement. "Just putting a new tape together; trying some new stuff," responded Atif, with a yawn. Atif picked up a cassette and handed it to Clement, "Here check this one out and tell me how you like it. Yo' when are you going to come back and work on that jam with me?"

"Let's do it tomorrow."

"Bet, I'm going to bed now."

"You look like you need to. I'll come check you out tomorrow."

"A'ight. Peace."

"Peace."

Clement left and returned to the street, turning the corner up to Burke Avenue – heading toward Gun Hill Road. He pulled a Walkman out of his inner jacket pocket and put Atif's tape into the compartment. The tape provided a soundtrack for his journey. Atif had been experimenting with mixes of jazz, hip-hop and old funk and soul records. It was a sound that people found to be weird, but Clement and some folks down in Greenwich Village thought it was cool.

Clement rounded the corner and crossed the street. As he walked to Gun Hill Station, he passed a Botanica/Bodega that had been there forever. Next door was a beauty supply shop that sold hair by the bag and an old record store with a speaker mounted into the door. The record store sold a lot of different types of music but seemed to specialize in West Indian music, particularly, Dance-hall Reggae. A Socca tune by Mighty Sparrow was blasting through the speaker. He passed a storefront law office where, according to the neon signs in the window, people could get divorces for $150. Next door to the station was a taxi company, where most of the night drivers were just getting off of work.

Gun Hill Station was an old, aboveground station, and Gun Hill Road became a bridge over the train tracks. He entered the ancient station doors and started to wait in line for a token. The token clerk, engrossed in deep conversation with a friend, was a heavy-set, brown-skinned woman with a bad extension job and a permanent expression of "attitude" on her face. A woman who wore a nurse's uniform under her coat and an elderly man stood on the line in front of Clement. "Once again, here is an example of somebody's job getting in the way of their social life," mused the old man in a crisp, Bajan accent. Just beyond the turnstiles and exit gate, there was a pair of dirty windows that over-looked the train tracks. Above the windows was a little box that held two protruding, bare light bulbs; one bulb was marked "TO THE CITY" and the other was marked "FROM THE CITY". The "TO THE CITY" light began to flash, but the token clerk didn't look like she was going to end her conversation at any time in the near future.

A Mixed Medicine Bag

The woman in front of Clement began to complain, but the token booth clerk ignored her and continued her conversation with her friend. Clement got off of the line, hopped the turnstile, and went down to the platform. The Five Train came rushing into the station and came to a noisy halt. The doors opened and a voice announced, "Gun Hill Station. The Numba' Five Train, making all local stops to 149th. and the Grand Concourse." Clement entered the car with the conductor.

The car was virtually empty except for a man wearing dreadlocks and dressed in all black who was reading a copy of *Black Skin, White Mask* by Franz Fannon. An elderly woman in a blue winter coat, with a large bag sitting between her legs on the train's floor also occupied the car. Clement fixed his gaze out of the window across from his seat and sank into the sounds being emitted from his Walkman. The 'boom' and 'bap' of the drums on his tape seemed to play a call and response game with the clacking sound of the train's metal wheels as they rolled over the tracks; the sound syncopated against the flashes of buildings that the train whirled past. Store signs, theater marquees, theaters-turned-churches, second and third floor apartments, projects, abandoned buildings, abandoned buildings being renovated, empty lots with mounds of dirt, athletic fields, ant-sized people and cars would flash by to the beat of the music.

After the Jackson Avenue stop, the train sank into the cavernous tunnel and made its way to the first underground stop on the train – 149th Street and 3rd Avenue. The next stop was his, 149th and the Grand Concourse. Clement liked this station because its round column posts and tile work on the walls still had an old fashioned look about it. He got off of the train and waited for the Two Train, which he would take to 135th Street Station. When he came out of that station, he would be next to Harlem Hospital on the corner of 135th and

Malcolm X Boulevard (Lenox Avenue). Clement crossed the street, passing the Schaumburg Library, an old soul food hole-in-the-wall take-out place, a bar that had a jazz organist, and walked up to 137th Street.

This was an extremely familiar route for Clement. He traveled this way every Saturday morning for the last three years for his saxophone lesson. During the five years prior to that, his father or mother drove him to the lessons. His teacher lived in a brownstone on 137th Street, one block in from St. Nicholas Avenue. Clement studied with a man named Drew Berris, who was also known as "The B Man". As Clement neared The B Man's house, he put his Walkman away, knowing that The B Man hated Walkmans. "Are you kids so afraid of your own thoughts that you have to block them out with mindless music?" the elder man would ask.

The B Man was 81 years old and 66 of those years were spent as a professional musician. He had been through the big band era, be-bop, progressive jazz, hard-bop and fusion as a musician, arranger and bandleader. The B Man was from Cincinnati, Ohio and was the son of a preacher. His father did not want him playing anything but church music, but The B Man had other ideas. He learned to play the saxophone from an old man who lived down the street from him. He had to keep his dreams so secret that he kept his sax hidden in an old tree in the woods near his music teacher's house. After school, The B Man would practice his music in the woods.

The B Man's music teacher was from New Orleans and was considered to be a "Conjure Man". People from the community would occasionally go to him with their problems, but The B Man's father considered the old man a devil-worshipper. "That old African stuff is the reason why there was slavery," his father would say, "God was punishing them for not following his word." The B Man's father would have had a heart attack if he found out that his son, as well as two-thirds of his congregation was going to the old man.

The old man had an old conga drum sitting in the front room of his house. He would tell The B Man about his youth in New Orleans, where drummers would come together and play and sing old African chants. This was believed to be the roots of New Orleans Jazz, where instruments imitated human voices and African rhythm patterns. The old man told The B Man that his goal as a musician was to use his instrument to imitate the sounds of nature, voices, animal sounds, the wind in the trees, doors creaking and things like that. The old man was an incredible musician, but could not read a note of music. The B Man learned to read music and the principles of music theory from the organist/choir director at his father's church. The B Man was able to keep this up for close to two years his before his father found out.

One afternoon, his father just happened to walk by the spot where The B Man would practice and heard his son playing. His father was furious and told The B Man, after a sound whipping, that he could not serve two masters. With that, The B Man joined the first jazz band that came through town – they were playing a high school dance and getting ready to hit the Chittlin' Circuit. The Chittlin' Circuit was a series of concert halls, night clubs and venues that ran up and down the east coast, starting in Philadelphia, down to Florida and back up to New York City. The B Man played with the band for three years, touring all over the country.

Life on the road caused the band to act like a family. He remembered the funny things that happened, like the time some guys in the band put exploding caps on the hammers of a dance-hall piano before a dress rehearsal – nearly scaring the piano player to death. Then there was the time that some of the guys in the band were tired of one of the trumpet players bragging about all of his women. One night, while playing in Macon, Georgia, they got this particular trumpet player drunk and got a transvestite to go up to his room with him. He didn't realize that he was making out with a man until he tried to go all the way. When somebody's birthday would come, it would turn into a weekend long party, complete with cake, candles, booze, women and reefer.

There were the not-so-fun times, like the time they saw the carcass of a man, hung by the neck and floating in the wind like a wind sock in a field. There was the time that a drunken sheriff and his "deputies" raided the hotel that the band was staying in because he heard that one of them had a white girl with him in the room. There was the night that one of the trombonists shot himself in the head when he got a letter that his wife was leaving him and was pregnant by another man.

When The B Man was eighteen, he left the band and joined the army. In the army he kept playing his sax, earned his G.E.D., and earned his way up to the rank of Staff Sergeant. When he got out of the army, he settled in New York City and went to City College, landing a job in the house band at Minton's Playhouse. When he finished college, he had a yearning to check out the scene in Europe where he heard that Blacks were having an easier time. So he saved up some money and traveled over to Paris, forming a small bebop combo and touring all over Europe.

It was during this period, that he acquired the name "The B Man". His band was premiering at a club in the Latin Quarter section of Paris called the "Caveau Heuchette". The M.C. was a Frenchman who had obviously hung around with Black musicians. When the M.C. gave his delivery, which was an obvious steal from Peewee Marquette, it ended with "An' now, eet ezz wit great pleasure zat I introduce, Drew 'Zee The B Man' Berris, and heez combo!" The B Man liked this so much that the name of the group became "The B Man's

Five." The B Man played alto and tenor sax, and his combo had a piano, bass, drums, and trumpet. Although he never received the large-scale recognition that Parker, Young, Coltrane and Coleman received, he was considered a musician's musician and made a good living touring Europe. While he was there, he was free from much of the racism that he remembered in America.

Feeling that he was missing very little in America, he stayed in Europe for nearly twenty-one years. When Medgar Evers was murdered, The B Man was in Paris. When Kennedy was shot, he was in Russia. When Malcolm X was killed, he was in Germany and had already earned a doctorate in music (for some reason, Europeans had much more respect for jazz than Americans did). When Martin Luther King Jr. was gunned down, he was in Italy. As far as The B Man was concerned, America held nothing for him but bad memories. In Europe, he had recorded over ten albums of his own and was a featured player on countless others.

In 1966, he had begun to hear about a thing happening in Harlem called the Black Arts Movement. This movement was similar to the Harlem Renaissance, with one little twist. The Harlem Renaissance was about a bunch of Black artists trying to emulate Europeans; but, the Black Arts Movement was a group of Black artists who were adamantly expressing Black culture and cultural influence, connecting their music, visual arts, theater, dance and literature to their African roots. The B Man found this encouraging – that, and the rise of a group called 'The Black Panthers'. At the tender age of sixty-two, The B Man made the move back to the U.S.A. to take part in the movement.

It was a big leap for The B Man to return to the U.S. as, except for some of the artists who had hung out in Europe or were true jazz aficionados, The B Man was virtually unknown in America. He bought a building in Harlem, moved in and started becoming active in the movement. He participated in a lot of the experimental projects and activities of the time. He refused several gigs in the downtown clubs, in keeping with the philosophy of the movement. Then, around the early to mid 1970's, the movement fell apart and The B Man was just another old Harlem musician. Since movements never pay very well, The B Man had spent a great deal of his savings. He was able to support himself by occasionally playing pick-up gigs around town, lecturing at City College and the Manhattan School of Music, and taking in private students. The B Man had a friend who lived in the Bronx who played African drums (Yusef's father). His friend had a neighbor whose son, Clement, wanted to take up the saxophone.

The B Man was in the kitchen when the bell rang. As usual, Clement was right on time. The B Man looked forward to his lessons with Clement as much as Clement did. Clement consumed music as if he was starving, a quality that The B Man appreciated. The B Man taught music the same way that the old man had taught him: playing, listening, analyzing, and playing some more. All sounds had a tone, texture, shape and quality that were to be appreciated; the arranging of these sounds was what created music. The B Man was a strong believer in the power of scales. For the first six months of studying with The B Man, Clement played nothing but scales. Clement would come to his lesson with a piece of music that the school band was working on, The B Man would look at it and give it back to Clement asking, "What key is it in?" Clement would answer and The B Man would ask, "What scales are in that key?" Clement would figure them out and name them, and then The B Man would have him play each scale. When he was finished, The B Man would say, "Good, now you know the song." Sometimes, he would give Clement a song in *Concert A* and make him transpose the tune into the key for saxophone. All of this helped to mold Clement into one of the best young musicians in the city. He won awards in city, regional and state music festivals and competitions.

Clement only paid for an hour lesson, but they usually lasted two and sometimes three hours. The B Man sensed a certain something about Clement and thought that there was a deeper spiritual reason why he was to be Clement's music teacher. Because of this certain something, The B Man felt that it was his duty to usher Clement in his development as a player. As part of his lessons, The B Man would play all kinds of records for Clement, including jazz, opera, African drumming and chanting, gospel, French folk music and old scratchy 78 blues records. Clement would share the mix tapes that he got from Atif with The B Man, who liked a lot of what he heard. Some of the rap records, particularly those by guys with names like KRS-ONE and Rakim, reminded him of The Last Poets and Gil Scott Heron. Most of the tunes that Clement worked on came out of "The Real Book", a popular book among jazz musicians that contained the chords and melodies to many jazz standards. Clement was expected to learn the tune and develop several improvised lines and new melodies over the chord progressions.

The B Man had noticed that Clement had gotten locked into a pattern of using scales and began encouraging him to use less linear approaches to the music. "Play the notes from other scales." he would tell Clement. To help break Clement of this habit, The B Man started playing a lot of Thelonius Monk, John Coltrane and Ornette Coleman recordings. For ear training, The B Man would give Clement a tape and have him chart out the sax lines. Clement would tease The B Man and say that he was making him do this because he was too lazy to write the charts himself. The elder would just look at him and say, "You're right – now get to work."

Today's lesson was like the others. Clement came in and they talked while The B Man drank his tea. Clement had

become so accustomed to playing scales at home; it was no longer a part of his lesson. He would play the prepared piece for The B Man and The B Man would record it. When he was done, his teacher would play the tape back and stop it to point out the places where Clement played particularly well and those places where he could have performed a little better. The lesson also always included Clement and The B Man playing a sax duet using melodies from jazz tunes, gospel music and some African chants that The B Man learned in his youth. One sax would play the melody and the other would sketch out the harmony lines with a counter-point melody. Today, The B Man decided to teach Clement a new tune, based on an old spiritual that came from a mix of African and Cherokee music. It was a rich tune that consisted of a lot of call and response sections. Clement was just getting into the tune when The B Man stopped playing.
"What's wrong?" asked Clement.
"Nothing, I just need a rest."
    Clement looked at his watch and realized that they had been at it for over three hours today. "We can call it quits for today." said Clement.
"Okay. I'll show you the rest of the tune next week." Responded The B Man.
    Clement realized that his teacher must have really been tired because he never wanted to call it quits. The B Man was sitting in his favorite chair – a big, overstuffed easy chair with a bright red cover. Most of his students referred to it as his throne. His sax sat resting upon its sax stand just to the right of the chair.
"Do you want another cup of tea?" asked Clement.
"Yes, thank you."
"Two teaspoons of sugar?"
"No. Honey, please."

Clement fixed the tea and brought it to The B Man, who thanked him and began to sip it slowly. His hands were shaking slightly as he held the cup. Clement waited around for a while to see if his mentor needed anything else. When The B Man assured him that everything was okay, he packed up his sax, music and left.

It seemed like a longer walk than usual to the train station that afternoon. The cold air was very still and Clement felt slightly light-headed. When he reached the steps of 135th. Street Station, he realized that he left his hat at The B Man's. He considered going back for it the following week, but something told him to return for it that day. He turned around and quickly walked back to The B Man's house. The B Man always gave his favorite students the key to his house; four years earlier he had given one to Clement. Although Clement never used the key, he carried it on his key ring with his own house keys.

When he got back to The B Man's house, he rang the bell. Nobody came to the door, so he rang again. When there was still no answer, he started to knock on the door. The B Man's music parlor was the front room on the first floor of the building and Clement was able to look into window. The B Man was still sitting in his chair, as if he were asleep. Clement, sensing something wrong pulled the key out of his pocket and let himself into his teacher's house. He ran into the parlor and gently shook the old man, who didn't move. Clement called an ambulance, which came almost an hour later. After checking the elder man, he was pronounced dead. The coroner said that the cause of death was a stroke caused by a heart attack – The B Man had slipped off into the next world.

Because The B Man had not left a will, his estate was given to distant cousins from Mississippi, who he never knew existed. They went through his belongings, sold most of his furniture to a collector, put the building up for sale and gave his saxophone and some of his records to Clement.

For close to three months, Clement never touched the sax, nor did he listen to the records that he inherited from The B Man. Then, late one April evening, Clement suddenly got an urge to pick up The B Man's sax. He took it up to the roof of his house and looked at it. The silver buttons shone in the glow of the sodium lights. Clement just stood there, with the sax in his hand, staring at it as though he was in a trance. It was a mild evening and a cool breeze started to blow through the budding tree branches as they slapped against the sides of his house. Finally, Clement lifted the sax to his lips, took a deep breath and began to play. The melody that flowed from the sax was unlike anything that he'd ever played before. There were points where it almost sounded like two saxophones, like the days when Clement and The B Man would blow a duet.

Clement closed his eyes and continued playing the unfamiliar and haunting melody. When he opened his eyes, he no longer saw his roof, the streetlights or the trees. All he saw were swirling patterns of purple, yellow, red, green, black and blue. The world around him had no shape, size, dimension or order. He could no longer feel the ground beneath his feet; it was as if he was floating in a swirl of colors and lights. Then, as he played, he could hear the low, gentle tones of The B Man's voice saying, "You've got it! Now take it somewhere..."

Energy, matter and consciousness cannot be created or destroyed; they can only change form. The place between asleep and awake has no such thing as birth, death, time or shape. It is the place where everything that ever was, is, and shall be co-exists. It is the place where all artists strive to be, but few ever reach.

~ Twelve ~

Lion's Magic

Many, many, many years had passed since the day that Lion was given a taste for blood. The strange, ape-like creatures that caused this had disappeared back into the mountains and hid in the darkness of their caves. People began to appear on the earth and slowly take control of the lion's domain, believing that their powers of logic, reason and speech made them superior to all of the other animals.

Although they were regarded as lesser beings, Lion's male descendants were "The Kings of the Beasts" and even people still had a healthy respect (spelled *f-e-a-r*) for the animals. As the lion's domain began to shrink, so did their access to necessary resources like food and shelter (lions were already born with clothing). Some humans promised them food, shelter and easy lives. Needing a way to feed themselves and their families, some of the lions jumped at the idea. They didn't realize that these promises translated into living in a cage and/or dancing for the amusement of other humans. Some people had gone so far as to capture lions and train them to do amusing tricks that any self-respecting lion would be too proud to ever perform. Even worse, some people would throw things at the lions.

Every now and again, a lion would reach his or her breaking point during one of these performances and attack their trainer or members of the audience. These lions always ended up being killed before they had a chance to fully stage their revolt. The suppression of attacking lion would always be carried out in front of the other lions as a way of letting them know "who was in charge" and what their fates would be if they decided to rebel. Yes, in many ways, the humans proved to be as bad, if not worse, than the strange, ape-like creatures who had tried to take control of the lion's dominion so many years before.

Years ago, lions had a mastery of logic, reason and communication; but, this ability to was lost to them due to in-breeding. In this generation, there was one lioness that still held the ability to think, reason, and even communicate with other animals. Now when I say communicate, I do not mean that she could verbalize; she had the power of mental telepathy and could communicate with other animals (and some people) through her thoughts.

One afternoon, a young prince had wandered outside the walls of the kingdom and into the jungles where the lions lived. His father was sick and it seemed as though the time for him to become king was rapidly approaching. Like many princes, this one was being educated by the Wise Man of the king's court – learning about practical knowledge (reading, writing and mathematics), abstract knowledge (logic, reason and empirical analysis), and intuitive knowledge (spirituality, dreams and senses). The prince's education would need to be accelerated, since he had not yet mastered all that was necessary for a king to know. The Wise Man told him that he would need to free his mind of all things that were familiar to him. This would mean leaving the kingdom to meditate. Hearing this, the young man wandered out of the kingdom toward the jungle, and was planning to go to the desert to meditate as the Wise Man suggested.

As the young man meandered through the jungle contemplating how he would meditate and how this meditation would help him, the lions sat and watched their potential meal draw closer and closer. The lioness caught a flash of what he was thinking and advised the other lions not to harm the tender young morsel. Knowing the young lioness to be wise and clever, the other lions grudgingly listened to her advice and allowed the young man to pass through the jungle unharmed.

The young lioness picked up on the fertile activity of the young man's mind and began to read his thoughts. He had read so many books and ingested so many ideas, that the lioness felt like a cub set loose in a field of sheep. Quietly, she followed the young prince through the jungle until he reached the desert and sat on a tall sand dune.

The young prince was trying to find this intuitive knowledge, but didn't know how would it come to him? Would there be a sign, a vision, a flash, or voices? The young lioness also picked up on these thoughts and decided to have a little fun. She sent the prince a message: *"What are you looking for?"* The prince looked around, startled. He heard the sweet and gentle voice of a woman, but saw no one.
"Who said that?" the prince thought to himself.
"It's me," replied the voice, "who do you think it is?"

As the prince began to think that he was going crazy, the lioness picked up on it and laughed to herself. "No, you are not going crazy. Sometimes, when we think really deeply, we are able to pick up on the thoughts of other deep thinkers." This made perfect sense to the young prince; his deep thoughts often lead to him reading the thoughts of his teacher and sometimes even the thoughts of his father. Of course, he thought of this as more of a coincidence than ability.

After introducing themselves to each other, the lioness and the prince began commiserating about how lonely it could sometimes be as the heirs to kingdoms. They discussed what it would mean to one day rule these kingdoms and all of the responsibility that it would entail. A few times, the lioness slipped and would make references to dens instead of palaces and cubs instead of children. At one point, when they were discussing hunting, the lioness accidentally talked about using her claws; however, she caught herself and was able to pass over it without the prince noticing.

These mental conversations continued for quite some time, with the prince regularly venturing through the jungle and out into the desert. One of the conversations focused on hair and the power that it holds. The young lioness used this as the opportunity to discuss the importance of a lion's mane. She talked about how the mane retained the thoughts, experiences and wisdom of the person who allowed it to grow. She told the young man how his mane (hair) would be one of his principle assets as a king and warrior. The lioness told the prince, *"Your hair is your magic. Think of the lion's mane. The lion is the King of the Beasts and ruler of the jungle – part of a lion's power is in his mane. A good, wise and powerful king always has a good mane... I mean, head of hair."* She told the prince that as his hair grew, he should have his servants rub his scalp with oils and juices from plants, and twist his hair until it locked. Then it would be like a lion's mane.

The prince did as he was told which often drew the mocking comments of his father and the rest of the royal family. As time went by, the prince's intuitive knowledge increased at a rate and to a level that astounded his teachers and even the king. He was able to sense and feel thoughts, ideas and feelings coming from people in the kingdom and those who would come to visit. The prince continued to venture through the jungle and into the desert. In seven years time, his hair was long and flowing down his back.

It was exactly seven years to the date of his first conversation with the lioness, that she revealed herself to the prince. The other lions stayed in the background, believing that the prince would see the lioness and run screaming. To their surprise, the prince was not afraid. In fact, he embraced the lioness as an old friend. As time continued, the prince and the lioness would sit in the desert together and roam through the jungles talking to each other through telepathy (and occasionally getting in a little hunting).

The lioness' eyes captivated the prince. Her eyes were a beautiful, deep shade of light brown, with flecks of gold. The light scar on the prince's left cheek also intrigued the lioness. He said it was a left over from his childhood – he had fallen out of a tree while playing. There was a troubling, unspoken reality that the prince and the lioness shared: over the years, they had fallen in love with each other. Needless to say, a lioness and a human prince could never be together in the way that they desired; however, each of them were being pressured by their parents because it was time that they found mates – any good ruler would need a partner to grow into the role with them.

One night, the prince sat in the courtyard of the palace, as the lioness sat out in the jungle – each of them looking at the waxing moon and thinking of the other and their years of friendship. The prince knew that the lioness was his soul mate and she echoed the sentiment. A lion and a human can never be together. This would be a romance that not only went against society's dictates, but would go against the very laws of nature – it could never be!

I'm not going to say that it was magic, nor am I going to say that it was a miracle. However, as the sun rose in the sky the next morning, a beautiful young woman approached the palace accompanied by a small court of servants. A king from a far off land had sent her as a potential bride for the prince; the prince was immediately summoned. When the prince reached the court, the most beautiful princess he'd ever laid eyes on greeted him. Curiously, the princess had a knowing smile on her face; but it was her eyes that were even more curious. They were a lovely shade of light brown with golden flecks, just like the lioness. The princess winked at him and he smiled back.

In the jungle, at the very same time, a young lion called on the lioness' father – the king – stating that he was seeking her as his mate. The king summoned his daughter to meet her suitor. When she arrived, she was introduced to the handsome young lion. Curiously, the young lion had a knowing smile and an interesting scar on the left side of his muzzle, just like the prince. The young lion winked at her and she smiled back.

Another five years passed and the prince was crowned "King Ras" (which means "Lion"). His hair was flowing and had grown to just below his waist. He had learned from his beautiful queen that when she was a girl, she had befriended a young lion. She would often remark on how much Ras reminded her of him. Meanwhile, deep in the jungle, the lioness and her mate ruled their domain together, while sharing similar tales (get it?). Each ruled their domains happily and wisely until they joined the ancestors. Again, I will call this neither magic nor miracle; but, I will say this: In all of the known history of the terrestrial and celestial world, soul mates who are meant to be together, shall be… no matter what.

~ Thirteen ~

The Society Secret

On a calm, autumn evening in the late 17th century, Eustace Randolph, the silversmith, strolled through the streets of the city, passing the many brick and wooden framed houses and shops that tightly lined the streets. He still had some time to kill before the meeting and he didn't want to get there too early. He had left his shop early that day, as it was impossible to concentrate with all of the excitement and anticipation about the upcoming meeting, as he lingered around the steps of the church. The Temple of The Society was about three blocks down from the church, and Eustace expected that tonight would be the night that his life was going to change forever. It would be the culmination of nine years of faithful study, proper, upright behavior, and regular involvement in benevolent causes. Finally, Eustace would be rewarded for all of his efforts.

The temple was a huge, three-story, gray, stone building with a tall tower in the middle. The tower's windows faced in all four directions. The main part of the building was about twenty-seven feet high, with four windows on each side at the very top of the main building. The tower stood approximately two stories above the roof of the main building. The front of the temple had two Dorian pillars and a gigantic, brass door. Over the door, carved into the stonework, was an inscription in a language that had long since been forgotten – at least by the common man. A rough translation would be the phrase, "For Those Who Dwell Within, Eternal Life Is Inevitable."

Next to the jail and the church (in that order), this temple was the oldest structure in the city.

As far back as anyone could remember, no one has ever seen the gigantic door open. Nor have they ever seen anybody enter or exit the building. There was a simple explanation for this. The actual entrance to the temple was a few blocks away. It could be reached through a secret compartment near the church's basement entrance, under the pipes of the organ. Two flights of winding stairs led to a long, stone tunnel that ran under several blocks of the city to another spiral staircase, just inside the temple's front door. Although everyone knew about the Society, nobody knew the particulars. There had been all kinds of rumors, and deep, dark tales about what went on in the society temple and how much power and influence The Society and its membership were presumed to wield in the city and in the world at-large. Because the membership was one of its secrets, nobody was exactly sure as to who the members of The Society were. It was rumored that they were men from all walks of life who had been deemed worthy by the elite of the order. The eldest citizen of the city might recall a time when a member of The Society admitted to being a member while in a drunken state one night in a tavern. Soon after, he mysteriously disappeared without a trace.

The only thing that could be made public was a man's desire to become a member. After careful and secret observations, if the candidate was deemed worthy, a sealed note would appear under his door that would instruct him to go – alone – to an alley just off of a street in the lower city. There, three men in black robes would appear and the candidate would be blindfolded and whisked away into the night to a cottage where he took an oath of secrecy, signed it, and sealed it with a drop of his blood. After receiving his first initiation rites, he was returned to the alley where he was instructed to count to 120 before removing the blindfold.

From that point, the candidate would receive lessons from the brotherhood on a weekly basis. Nothing was ever written down. After passing each exam given him by the brotherhood, the candidate would advance to the next rite, approximately three rites per year.

The mysteries of the order were based in the legends of King Faruq, the ancient, benevolent, and wise ruler who turned knowledge into gold. The temple, itself, was modeled after the temple that King Faruq was said to have built on the eastern side of his palace. Faruq's temple was said to be the original university of the land where initiates would be secretly selected, whisked away from society and required to take an oath of secrecy. There, for the next nine years, they would study under the masters and high priests, learning the twenty-seven sacred degrees of the universe. According to the legends of The Society, they were the keepers of this arcane knowledge and their power was infinite because of it.

Eustace remembered the ritual of his ninth degree (which the society called his Born degree), which took place on the first level of the temple. It was a re-enactment of the rise of King Faruq. Eustace had to remove his clothing, drape himself in a diaper-looking piece of linen and get into a black box. The box was placed into a flume and sent traveling along a channel that twisted and turned. At the end of the ride, his diaper was replaced with the clothes of a poor farmer. He was placed into the middle of the Circle of Contemplation, where the four directions were marked with symbols. Then, after giving a password that he learned from an old woman (played by Brother Walker, the grocer), he had to pass through the chamber of the three blind giants and obtain a lock of hair from each of their heads. At the end of the ritual a crown was placed on his head.

MWALIM '7)

He thought back to the night that he received his eighteenth degree (Knowledge Build-Destroy degree). This time it was a re-enactment of King Faruq's nameless descendant. The ritual took place on the second level of the temple. Eustace had to put on the clothing of a peasant, and travel through the chambers of mistreatments, guided by a wise old man (played by Brother Walker, the grocer). The chamber occupants (played by Bros. Jones, Winslow,

Garrison, Waters, Hill, Walcott, Brixton...) cursed and spat upon him as he passed. After passing through the chamber of slavery, Eustace was given the clothing and weapons of a warrior. He then had to remove the sacred black box from the chamber of liberation and burn the city (a miniature model).

Before qualifying for his final step, the twenty-seventh degree (Wisdom God degree), Eustace had to take a long and involved oral exam. He had to know the answers perfectly and from memory. Again, nothing was ever written down.

Q: Where did King Faruq have his temple built?
A: On the eastern side of his palace.
Q: Why did he have it built on the eastern side of the palace?
A: Because he enjoyed watching the sunrise over the tower.
Q: Of what was the walkway leading from the palace to the temple constructed?
A: Stones shaped as bricks and carefully placed in mortar.
Q: How long and wide was the walkway?
A: 528 cubits long and 14 cubits wide[5].
Q: Where did the walkway begin and where did it end?
A: It began at the eastern gate of the palace and ended at the front door of the temple.
Q: It is said that King Faruq went to the temple everyday, but no one ever saw him enter or exit the building. How is this possible?
A: There was a secret compartment, just inside of the eastern gate of the palace, with a winding staircase that led to a tunnel. The roof of the tunnel was the visible walkway between the palace and the temple.

---

[5] About 3 blocks long by 21 feet wide

The tunnel led to the ground level of the temple, just inside the front door.

Q: How tall was the temple?

A: The main building of the temple was 28 cubits high. The tower was an additional 54 cubits, making the whole structure 82 cubits in height.

Q: How many levels did the temple contain?

A: The main building consisted of three levels. The tower consisted of a winding staircase, with two chambers at the very top.

Q: How many chambers and compartments were contained in the temple's main building?

A: 63.

Q: What were these chambers said to contain?

A: The chambers contained the wisdom of the ages.

Q: Upon receiving your first twelve degrees, what were you given with each degree?

A: With each degree, I was given a jewel.

Q: What were the jewels?

A: Food, clothing, shelter, knowledge, wisdom, understanding, freedom, justice, equality, love, peace, and happiness.

Q: What was contained within the tower and it's two chambers?

A: The chambers were said to be the inner sanctum of the temple. Legend has it that this is where the wise elder, from whom Faruq received his lessons, resided.

Q: What was his title and who is said to represent him in modern times?

A: He was King Faruq's Grand Visor and in modern times he is represented by the Omni-Potentate.

Q: Describe the chambers of the tower.

A: One chamber was contained within the other. The outer chamber was said to be the Grand Visor's living

> space. The inner chamber was the place where he gave King Faruq his lessons.
> Q: What sits in the center of the inner chamber?
> A: An altar with a black box resting upon it.
> Q: Were did the box come from?
> A: The box was made, by the order of King Faruq, from the black wood found in Pelan – also called Patmos.
> Q: What is said to be the contents of that black box?
> A: The secret teachings and laws of universal knowledge. King Faruq wrote down the lessons that he received from the wise elder on linen and carved the secret universal law on a piece of wood. He wrapped the lessons around the stick and placed them in the box.

After experiencing the final ritual, Eustace was presented with a rectangular, black box that was encrusted with five-pointed stars made of gold. The lecturer, who was also the Thrice-Illustrious, Immediate-Past, Omni-Potentate (Bro. Winslow, the banker) explained to Eustace, in a post-initiation lecture that this black box contained the ancient secrets of universal knowledge. At last, Eustace was a 'Keeper of the Ancient Secret'. He was instructed to never open the box under any circumstance and told to **put** it in a safe place where he would always be able to protect it. The lecture concluded and the brotherhood prepared for a celebration.

"But, what is the secret?" Eustace inquired of the Grand Omni-Potentate (Bro. Kendall, the baker).
"Just that – a secret." replied the Grand Omni-Potentate.
"How can I keep a secret that I don't know?"
"Well, if you don't know the secret, you'll never be able to reveal it. By keeping the box sealed and protected, you're keeping the secret."

Eustace got home after the celebration and took the box from his inner coat pocket, shaking it gently. Something inside of it rattled. He placed the box on the mantle of his study and tried to forget about it. After three days of trying to forget, he couldn't stand it anymore. Using his letter opener, he pried the box open in such a way that he could replace the small wooden panel and its nails. Inside, he found several small pieces of parchment rolled around a stick and held with a red ribbon. Eustace carefully removed the ribbon and unrolled the pieces of paper. The paper was blank but the stick had words carved on it:

WE TOLD YOU: "IT'S A SECRET"

Eustace took the stick, wrapped the parchment back around it, tied the red ribbon back onto the parchment, placed it all back in the box. After carefully replacing the wooden panel, he put it back on the mantle in his study. He then went to his window and looked out at the moonlit temple cutting through the night sky. Suddenly, he darted from the window to the mantle, snatched the box, and flung it into the fire. He watched it burn as the flames turned the black box into ashes and the stars melted into the flames. He thought long and hard about the last nine years of his life: the sacrifices he'd made, the hours, days, and weeks of studying, the indignities of some of the rituals – just to have it all turn out to be a joke. He did, however, take solace in the fact that new applications for membership had been made and he would soon be able to take part in the initiations.

About three weeks later, an envelope was slipped under Eustace's door. It looked a lot like the one that he received nine years earlier. He opened and read it:

A MIXED MEDICINE BAG

GREETINGS MY GOOD BROTHER!

I PRAY THAT THIS LETTER FINDS YOU IN GOOD HEALTH. PLEASE ACCEPT THIS AS NOTICE THAT OUR NEXT REGULAR MEETING WILL TAKE PLACE ONE WEEK FROM TUESDAY AT OUR REGULAR TIME.

AGAIN, CONGRATULATIONS ON YOUR ASCENSION. REMEMBER THAT AS THE NEWEST BROTHER, YOU ARE RESPONSIBLE FOR THE POST-MEETING COLLATION. WE LOOK FORWARD TO YOUR REGULAR ATTENDANCE.

UNTIL WE MEET AGAIN.

Bro. Malcolm Walcott

SACRED GRAND SCRIBE & SCROLL BEARER
- THRICE-ILLUSTRIOUS, SUPREMELY ADEQUATE YET, TWICE-REVERED JUNIOR ELDER PAST OMNI-POTENTATE
- WELL PAST SUPREMELY-EXCELLENT, MASTER HIGH PRIEST OF THE SEVEN REALMS

P.S. — Shame on you for cooking in the box. Yet, take heart in the knowledge that most of us have done the same thing. If you would ever care to replace the box that I'm sure you've destroyed by now, it can be procured through the Reasonably-Excellent High Priest, Brother Jones.

Storyteller's Note: Brother Walcott owned the printing shop and Brother Jones was the cabinetmaker.

EPILOGUE:

According to oral history, the box did, at one time, contain the scrolls of Faruq, wrapped around the walking stick of the wise elder. On the walking stick was carved the secret opening of a particularly powerful prayer. About 430 years later, the box was removed from the temple when the city was raided. It later emerged in the home of a Duke whose wife decided to use the "linen with the curious patterns" as shades for their country home.

The Duke's valet, who was a student of the Classics and dabbler in the esoteric and occult, recognized the scrolls and knew that the "curious patterns" were ancient scriptures. In secret he studied, translated and transcribed them. Once he had memorized the words on the stick, he threw the stick into the fire – deciding that he would only reveal the secrets to those who were worthy. He died before he could find anyone worthy of sharing the secret with. His manuscript ended up as packing materials for some of his belongings until another scholar came upon nine of his chapters and was able to surmise that there were about eighteen chapters missing. He supposedly recovered the missing information from an African merchant who said that the blessings of King Faruq were common knowledge in his land. After killing the African merchant, the scholar went about building temples throughout Europe. As for the secret words and powerful prayer, some say they mysteriously emerged in the African-American community in the mid-1960's and are still a part of the culture's slang that can sometimes be heard as a song, sung by little girls playing Double-Dutch.

~ FOURTEEN ~

YUSEF'S GROOVE

Intro:
December, 1989 - Northeast Bronx, NY

A cold wind blew on that gray morning when Yusef stepped out of his parent's house and strolled over to Baychester station. He didn't feel like walking up to Gun Hill that morning. It was the beginning of winter break and he had only been back in the Bronx for about three days. His old roommate, Atif, was living across town, on the west side. They had hung out the night before, having dinner and a few drinks to celebrate this occasion: Yusef embarking into the music industry.

"What the hell?" Yusef softly uttered, while facing the little black and white fare sign that hung over the token booth. The subway fare had gone up to $1.15. Why would they set the fare at such a weird rate? Baychester Avenue Station was much cleaner, and better lit than he remembered it being in his teens. In those days, the token booth clerk was more of an ornament, in that most of the younger subway riders refused to pay the fare and would walk defiantly through the subway exit door before striding up the staircase to the train platform. Times had changed. Now, even the smaller subway stations had under-cover cops sitting in the stations and/or up on the platforms. Not to mention the fact that the exit doors had electro-magnetic locks that held them in place unless a person was exiting or the token booth clerk pushed a button to let them through.

He stepped inside of the station, and decided to wait downstairs near the steaming radiator until the "To The City" light came on. It's funny, even after five years of living in Boston, that good old Northeast Bronx wind could still chill you to the bone. The light came on and the rattle of the train cars could be heard rapidly approaching. Yusef and the other passengers who chose to escape the cold platform by standing near the radiators, made their way up the steps to the approaching train. On the platform was a lone figure in a hoodie, way down near where the front of train stopped, leaning against the wall with his backpack serving as a cushion. The distinct aroma of a blunt was a clue as to why this young brother was willing to challenge the cold in waiting for the train. Not too far from him, some squirrels played in dried up, old leaves, while others ate the remnants of a Hostess apple pie. It was a "Red Five", which meant it was an older train and the cars would have heat. The heating systems on the old red trains were ridiculous. It would be 25 degrees outside, but about 70 in the train car.

Back when Yusef was in high school, he rode the train to school with his buddy Ossie. Ossie used to carry an attaché case that he swore was real leather. One day, when he sat down on the train, Ossie put his bag behind his legs (where it rested against the train radiator grate). By the time they got to 149th Street, one side of the case had melted slightly, with the grill pattern branded onto the side of the bag. Yet another "pleather rouse" had been uncovered.

For Yusef, this was going to one of many historic Five Train rides. He was on his way to the pressing plant in Brooklyn to press and package his first record. In his right hand he carried a black portfolio that contained camera-ready artwork and a small brown envelope containing a DAT, carefully labeled as "Valley Park Groove." It was actually a copy of the original DAT. With the advent of digital, Yusef never gave up his original masters if he could help it. As was his habit, he got on the subway car with the conductor, found a seat and settled in for a long train ride to Park Slope. The last three weeks had brought him a series of sleepless nights before deciding to make this move.

Head (Principle Melody):
May 1989 - Boston, MA

It was about a week after Yusef's graduation. Atif and Yusef had been sitting back on a Sunday afternoon in their Dale Street apartment, sipping wine and listening to some new records that had come in from the record pool. Along with the selection of house music, hip-hop, and R&B remixes, came some imported cuts. There was some very African drumming oriented stuff called Afro-beat, remixes and loops of old sixties records over drum machines called Rare-Groove, and some funky, seventies sounding stuff from London called Acid Jazz. The two young men sat, listening and grinning at each other. Back in the early eighties, they used to get together and jam in Atif's mother's basement. Atif, Yusef, Clement, and Barry, who played bass, would get together and play all afternoon, often recording what they came up with on Atif's four-track. Yusef would teach them his original tunes; this weird stuff where Yusef would play avant garde jazz riffs and chord voicings on the keyboard over Atif's break-beat records (the ones with the octopus on the label); as Clement would riff out the melody and Barry would play funky versions of Mingus-flavored acoustic bass lines. Yeah, now there was a place for that *weird stuff!* "I can do this." Yusef told Atif.
"Yeah, you can, but check the production quality on this compared to the stuff on your tapes."
"What are you talking about?" asked Yusef.

"Listen really carefully to what's happening on those tracks."

Yusef sat back, closed his eyes, and listened. Atif got up, stopped the record, dug out a cassette and popped it into the player. He switched back and forth from the tape to the record.

"See the quality difference?"

"Yeah. Those cats are cheating."

"Yup. But they sound perfect. That's why they're on vinyl."

Yusef nodded his head. He made a tape of some of the records and spent the next couple of weeks listening to it on his headset and analyzing the production.

Saturday evening, on the next to last week of June, Yusef had a date with Sandra – an MBA student at Harvard from Maryland. The date went well and they parted company on Sunday afternoon after lunch. He promised to call her on Monday. The sun began to sink into the Jamaica Way as Yusef walked through the Fenways, up Boylston Street towards Massachusetts Avenue. On the block of Boylston Street, just between Ipswich Street and Massachusetts Avenue, on the same block as Jack's Drum Shop, there's a pizza parlor called Little Steve's. In the basement of Little Steve's is a recording studio that you have to enter through the alley in back. Yusef worked there, having worked his way up from intern to staff engineer. As a freshman, he interned for a week at a studio in Roxbury owned by a big-time producer with a lot of major label bands. There was something about the vibe there that just didn't feel right, so he quit. A couple of weeks later it was a chance session with a classmate, who needed Yusef to play piano on a demo, that brought him to this little studio located around the corner from his school. They needed an intern and the rest is history. He spent a lot of his non-class and non-student job time in this studio, emptying ashtrays, picking up beer bottles and food bags, and helping to set up mics for sound checks. He also got to watch the engineers and producers do their thing in the control both, learning the ins and outs of the craft. Initially, Yusef was at Berklee as a jazz piano major, but soon switched to music production and business.

He walked the downward sloping alley until he reached a heavy, black, metal door. Yusef unlocked the door and stepped inside. One of the advantages of being a staff engineer was that you could record your own work during off hours; it was one of the perks offered by the studio's owner since he couldn't pay his staff a lot of money. Yusef turned on the equipment and pulled an Alesis SR-16 drum machine out of his backpack. Then he began to hook it up to the Mac's MIDI bay, plugging the four cables into the back of the machine and the other ends into the soundboard. After some more adjustments, he fired up the drum machine, recording the pattern onto the computer.

Ca
Boom-ba click, boom-click-boom, click, ca
Boom-ba click, boom-click-boom, click, ca
Boom-ba click, boom-click-boom, click, ca
Boom -------------------------------------- ca

Yusef reached into his backpack, pulled out a hand-held cassette recorder, went into the drum booth and recorded a bunch of drum riffs that were played against a click track.

Boom tick, tick, rat-boom-tat, click,
Boom-bap, shu-click, boom, ba-tat
Boom, Rat-tat-tat-, boom pataki, ah-boom
Boom, Rat-tat-tat-, boom pataki, ah-boom
--- Pataki-ah-boom, ah, boom, bap, bap, bap-bap-bap-bap-bap
Shu-shew, click, click, click, Pataki – boom

Then he went back into the booth and played the cassette into a sampler. Recording the drums on the little hand-held, designed for dictation and lectures, gave them that dirty, old recording sound that Yusef was looking for. With some cutting, pasting, and adjusting, he created loops out of the sampled drum patterns that fit into time with the drum machine pattern.

He picked up the acoustic bass that sat in the corner of the main room, plugged it into the soundboard, and recorded a series of jazzy sounding bass lines onto studio's 16-track tape deck against the drum patterns,

Duuuuuuuuuuuuuuuh, deee-dun
Doom, du-dolodune, dooo, beeeeeeee-baaaa
Doom, du-dolodune, dooo, beeeeeeee-baaaa----
Doom, doom, doom, dudududud.dolodooon
Doom, du, doom, du, doom, du, dooooooooooom
Dooooooooooooom, baaa-beeeee, du, dododoo, duh

He could have recorded this at school; but, then everybody would have been in his business and those European know-it-alls and super by-the-book techies would have wanted to tell him how he *should* do it. Stories circulate that Keith Jarred was kicked out of Berklee for retuning a piano; and years later, even at a jazz institution, folks were still scared of experimentation. Unbeknownst to Yusef, this experiment was about to become a defining moment.

Sax Solo:
September 1981 - Northeast Bronx, NY

Pataki-ah-boom, ah, boom, boom, boom,
click, click, click, pataki – boom
Rat-tat-tat-tat-tat, boom pataki, ah-boom

A Mixed Medicine Bag

Pataki-ah-boom, ah, boom, boom, boom,
click, click, click, pataki – boom
Rat-tat-tat-tat-tat, boom pataki, ah-boom

A few curious folks stopped to watch and listen to Mr. Bey's drum circle of students from the New World Arts Academy, as they jammed in Valley Park. It was still warm outside and a nice day, so Mr. Bey (Baba), decided to hold his advanced African drumming class in the park rather than in the studio. Yusef, Ian, and Clement had just finished their rite of passage into the advanced group, having learned the lesson of the drum from Baba. All of the students called him that; it is the term for father in several African cultures. In real life, he was Yusef's father. Yusef learned at an early age that he would have to share his father with all of the young artists who came through the academy, many of whom came from fatherless households. Sharing didn't bother him; in fact it made him proud. This made Clement and Ian more like brothers or close cousins then just best friends. They were that *walk-in-your-house-and-open-your-fridge* kind of close.
Rat-tat-tat-tat-tat, boom pataki, ah-boom
Pataki-ah-boom, ah, boom, boom, boom

There were five levels that student drummers had to pass through, culminating with their inclusion in the circle at around the age thirteen or fourteen. During these levels, Baba made all of his students study African drums regardless of what other instruments they studied. Clement played the sax and flute and Yusef played the piano and a little bass. Ian was the only one who was serious about drums and percussion, playing a trap-drum kit. Yusef and Clement had just begun their freshmen years at Music & Art High School in Harlem, up on 135th Street and St. Nicholas Terrace. Ian was down at Murray Bergtram.

Click, click, click, pataki – boom
Rat-tat-tat-tat-tat, boom pataki, ah-boom

Baba would talk extensively on the history, purpose, and evolution of drumming and the drum in the African Diaspora. "Jazz, Rock & Roll, Blues, Gospel, R&B, Soul, Hip-Hop, Reggae, Zook, Calypso… doesn't matter; it's all from the drum." He would add, "It doesn't matter what instrument you're playing, if the music is rooted in West African traditions, you're playing a drum… a rhythm… piano, guitar, vibes, organ, bass… they are all just tonal drums… The harmonies, too… the melodies were contributed by our Native ancestors… imitations of the sound of nature on flutes, saxophones, trumpets, violins, cellos, the voice…" Once Baba got started, he just flowed with it.
Pataki-ah-boom, ah, boom, boom, boom,
Click, click, click, pataki – boom

A small group of Boriquen men stood to the side and watched with a mix of scrutiny and silent admiration, as this circle of Moreno child master drummers played. The session finished and Baba brought the circle together for their closing ritual. In the reflection portion of the ritual, Ian said that he had some news to share with everyone. "I was looking for a new name and this one came to me by way of my grandmother. From now on, I'm to be called 'Atif'…" Baba smiled, "Atif. Nice name… do you know what it means?"
"No," replied Ian/ Atif, "what does it mean?"
"That's for you to discover. The taking on of a new, spiritual name is a big honor and responsibility. Welcome to the journey, Atif."
The rest of the class repeated the new name. Taking on a spiritual name was not required by the academy – nor was it even encouraged – but it was supported if it happened. Baba

poured the libation and then supervised the group in packing the drums before leading the procession up Hammersley Avenue towards the academy.

Melodic Reprise:
June 1989 – Boston, MA

Atif was on his way back to New York to try his luck at getting in with a record company as an A&R or promotions person. Since he hadn't done any internships in the industry, he had no set inroads. This meant that he would have to try to slip into the industry through his contacts who promoted records at the record pools, fishing through mailroom jobs, and possible leads that his godfather, Marshall, would give him. He had a couple of connections in the business. Atif spent his summer D.J.ing at clubs and undergrounds, working for his father, and visiting his mother and grandmother back in the Bronx. He was ready to bounce back to New York, especially since he and his father weren't speaking to each other... again.

Yusef, on the other hand, planned to remain in Boston for another couple of years, deciding to pursue a master's degree in music education (with a focus in composition) at the New England Conservatory. While Atif was moving out of the apartment on Dale Street, Yusef was preparing to live by himself for the first time in his 21 years. He was also going to try to swing the $475 a month in rent (plus utilities) on his own. He had his job at the studio and a couple of private piano students... mom and dad always mailed him a little something, so he'd be able to get by.

Clement decided to come up and visit his old buddies, Atif and Yusef. Atif had just graduated from Boston University and Clement had just finished Howard University. After years of adventures together, their little warrior band was about to embark on new ones. In July, Clement was about set out on a nine-month tour with this drummer from DC who arranged gigs all over the world through some federal program. He needed a good alto sax and flute player; and, of course, Clement was very excited about this prospect. Especially since he'd be playing in cities and venues that, when he was younger, "The B-Man" used to tell him about and show him pictures of.

Clement and Yusef grabbed a couple of subs and sodas at the pizza parlor on Boylston Street, before rounding the corner to go down into the studio. Clement had his sax slung over his shoulder as he and his buddy entered the subterranean studio and warmed it up for a recording session. Yusef had given Clement a cassette of the basic beat, chord and melody of the tune, muting out the experimental tracks. He didn't want them to color Clement's interpretation of the tune. Clement was also used to how Yusef liked to control the flow of spontaneity in the music, the way Miles Davis did on *Bitches Brew*, not letting the right hand know what the left was doing. For Clement, the bottom line was that Yusef wrote some interesting stuff and his production work on Clement's demo led to his getting the gig he has now. Because of this, his best friend's quirks meant very little to him.

Clement tuned up and warmed up his sax. They played a couple of pass-throughs for sound levels and then they recorded some sax and flute tracks. In a couple of hours, Yusef was happy with what they got. "When do I get to hear the final masterpiece, maestro? " Clement asked. "In a due time, Bird. In due time." Yusef replied, as he began shutting down the studio – putting away cords, packing away the reel-to-reel tape from the multi-track, and shutting down the computer after saving his sequences on disk. Yusef and Clement had been calling each other Maestro and Bird since high school.

A Mixed Medicine Bag

A couple of weeks later, on a hot July night, Yusef slipped back into the studio and played with the sampler. He selected his favorite bass lines, conga, and bongo patterns for the bridges and choruses. He added his favorite chords and vocal harmonies of the hook for the choruses and bridge, and kept the favorite takes of organ, piano, guitar, vibe, flute, and sax solos. Once all of the tracks were pristine, he went about the task of mixing it all down. Iris, an old friend who used to hang out and sing with the band at Connolly's, sang most of the vocals – creating a nice texture against Yusef's tenor and baritone passes. Thanks to automated boards, Yusef was able to save all of the settings for the mix onto a computer disk. He ran off a reference copy of the tune onto a cassette. In the first week in August, Yusef returned to the studio with Atif, his trusty DJ buddy, and they had a final mix: A full 9:52 version and a 3:09 radio version for side A, and a 4:10 lounge mix, 4:03 Afro-Latin Mix (using an alternate *montundo* piano and Afro-Cuban bass track), and a 4:12 Hip-Hop mix featuring a local poet on side B, which gave the track a Gil Scott-Heronesque flavor.

The streets vibrate with a pulse and a thud...
Valley Park greets the rising sun
It could be the heartbeat of the universe
Multi-colored swings, ball courts,
bicycle paths, and an outdoor pool
Valley Park comes alive
It's called a groove
A groove
To the sound of the trucks making deliveries
And the streets that come alive in the morning
My landscape
This is my world of the rising sun
The sound, the sound, the sound

Of a Valley Park morning
It's called a groove
A groove
Or is it just plain old background noise?
When you live in a circle
All things repeat themselves
There is still variation
And contradiction
In it's uniformity
This contradiction within uniformity
It's called a groove
A groove
Valley Park is alive
My first breath came after I entered the light
Each time I enter a new light, I breathe for the first time
My heart-beat came long before I could see
I had life before I could live
When a child is born
The elders will say
That an ancestor has returned
And the sun shall rise
Over Valley Park
It's called a groove
A groove
My connection to the earth is like no other
But all life can spring from the earth
And be sustained by her bounty
But that is only half of what makes you who you are
Look for the rest in the spirits of the skies
Over Valley Park
It's called a groove
A groove
When everything is moving,
it gives the illusion that everything is standing still

beauty evolves from the mistakes that we make
trying to repeat our past perfections
and this contradiction
is what we call a groove

By sunrise, "Valley Park Groove" was a finished product with three DAT copies.

Piano & Flute Solo:
September, 1989 - Bronx, NY

...All things repeat themselves
There is still variation
And contradiction
In it's uniformity
This contradiction within uniformity
It's called a groove

From a copy of Dance Music Report and the records in Atif's crates, Yusef was able to compile a sizable list of small labels that specialized in dance music like his. Atif made a couple of calls through his contacts in promotion and got Yusef a bunch of meetings. He remembered the first label that he visited was upstairs from an East Village record store. They sat in the cramped little office and listened to the tape together.

"I'll give you eeleven 'undred bucks for eet." said the skinny, trendy-looking, white boy, after exhaling a stream of clove cigarette smoke. He was dressed in a form-fitting turtleneck shirt and wore a goatee and five o'clock shadow.

"As an advance?" inquired Yusef?

"Total. To buy thee track outright. It's vary nize, but eet eez going to be 'ard to market."

"I could lease it to you."

"That would be a waste of time and money. I market thee track, get eet out there on thee turn tables and you take eet to a bigar company... no, I would 'ave to own eet."

"The master?"

"Well, yez, and thee pub-lisheeng, too."

Yusef took back his tape, thanked the man for his time and went on to the next label. They passed on the project, as did the label after that, and the label after that. The next label liked it, but wanted the publishing to this song and everything Yusef wrote for the next five years. The next six labels after that all wanted to make a deal like the first one, buy the track and song outright and send Yusef home with a couple of hundred to a couple of thousand bucks – what a rip off.

Later that night, Yusef and Atif sat in a bar on the corner of Boston Road and 222nd Street, talking about their fruitless efforts. Atif thought for a minute. "You know, we could press it up and pump it ourselves. I'm learning the ins and outs of this business."

"By hanging posters?" Chuckled Yusef.

"Yeah, *nig-row*. And from going to clubs and industry parties, and handing out records to every DJ in town – and servicing the record pools."

"Hmmmm."

"We could make this your calling card. Just get it marketed and promoted right.... Yeah, let's start a label."

Bridge - Breakdown:
October 1989 - Boston, MA

It was a crisp, autumn afternoon as Yusef and Sandra sat in his bedroom. He watched as Sandra crunched out a business plan – bringing together demographics, target markets, areas, methods of distribution, promotion, revenue, and long-term sustainable planning. *Liberation Records* was going to be a limited liability record company specializing in underground dance music. A part of their model would be the production of records and the other half would be licensing imported masters and marketing them in the USA. As seed money, Yusef cashed in the CD that he'd been building in the bank since he was fourteen and had a summer job. By that time, it was up to $6,000. Atif put up two grand and got his godfather to kick in two grand, as well. Sandra hit the print button and the seven-page document was finished. She went over it with Yusef, explained the particulars. She described how the document is used to attract investors, how you could only have 100 units to sell in a limited partnership, and so on. Sandra had decided to make *Liberation Records* her master's thesis. She signed on as a business manager, as an in-kind investment, making her a fourth partner.

Yusef's head was spinning. He went from simply wanting to make a record to owning... co-owning a record label that was going to need office space, studio budgets and/or equipment, storage space, distribution deals, invoices, legers, paperwork... Maybe he should have taken the $2,750 offered by that label in Long Island City, and kept making records to build up his reputation. Instead, this venture would be costing him money and time. Now Sandra was up under him a lot more, which was actually kind of cool; but, after not trying to have a girlfriend, he now had a business partner who liked sleeping in his bed. Yes, that Sunday in June brought him more than he bargained for. *Sigh.*

Melodic Reprise:
December 1989 – Brooklyn, NY

As Yusef walked along a rather deserted 3rd Avenue, the cold wind there felt like it did when he would walk along the

Charles in the winter. There were just a row of warehouses and factories on this street. He rounded the corner and came to a red metal door with a buzzer, rang the buzzer and stepped in. Yusef sat at the desk with the sales manager, who looked over the artwork, nodding in approval. The Liberation Records logo was simple – a triangle that held a silhouette of a trio playing drums, keys and sax within. The color version of the logo had the keyboards black on red, the drummer red on black, and the sax black on green. Sandra had convinced him to spend the extra $700 on a cover for the single, arguing that folks who recognized the cover make 18% of all record purchases. A cover would help it to stand out in the record bins, as well. This cover was a black and white photo of Yusef, playing a bass in Valley Park for an audience of attractive young women. The sky faded into a silhouette of Clement playing the saxophone and hands on the keys of a piano. In scratch graffiti, were the words *"Valley Park Groove - maxi-single- The Bass Mint Brothers"* The black and white photo was overlaid with red and green, creating a red, black, and green effect for the cover, too. He was also going to have them pressed onto green vinyl. The green symbolized parks, prosperity, and health.

    The sales manager took Yusef on a tour of the plant. The master tape was played through an amp that drove a needle to cut sound into a plate. The plate was used to make a die-cast metal mold called *stampers*. Then, the stampers are cut in half, placed on a machine where a molten blob of vinyl called a *biscuit,* is placed between two labels, forced between the stampers, soaked in cold water, and trimmed. BINGO! – a vinyl record is made.

    Since Yusef had an appointment, he got to watch his test pressing get made. These were the records that were pressed to listen to and determine whether or not the record needed to be re-cut. The sales manager showed him into a little room with a stereo and a bunch of speakers of various types... home stereo speakers, car speakers, subwoofers... all of the kinds of ways that the music would be heard. Yusef closed his eyes and listened. A smile formed on his face as he clicked through the different speakers. This was the record. Atif told him to get about 200 test pressings, as several of his club and underground DJ connections loved getting records that weren't out yet. He also ordered 2,000 white labels, in plain, black jackets for college radio and record pools and 5,000 fully packaged copies for everyone else (retail, reviewers, agents, etc.).

Later that night, Yusef and Atif must have hit about 20 nightclubs between the Bronx and Manhattan. Because Atif seemed to know everybody, and all of them knew him, they were granted immediate admittance to the clubs, handshakes and hugs from managers and DJs, and free drinks at the bars. Most importantly, the record would get slipped into the mix while they were still at the club. Yeah, for a poster hanger, Atif had something going on.

Piano Solo:
March – May 1990 - Boston, MA & The Road

The Hub Club was packed with folks. The Liberation Records release party was well-promoted and the fact that the club got double-booked the same night, by a drag queen fashion show, didn't hurt either. Yusef performed "Valley Park Groove" live with two drummers, a bass player, auxiliary keyboards, and a sax/ flute player. They cranked through a set that included funked-up versions of jazz standards, like "I Mean You," "Round Midnight," and "A Night In Tunisia." They were able to hand out several copies to D.J.s in the club, including the D.J.s from WERS, WILD, WRBB, WHRB, WFNX, and WMBR, many of whom posed for pictures with Yusef. The next three months were going to be hectic. He had a bunch of local promo gigs around New England and New York City.

In April, things picked up. Yusef took a leave of absence in his second semester to embark on a twelve-city tour. Sandra was able to help him get an agent – a small, hungry agency located in one of those small buildings in the 20's along Broadway. They got Yusef a tour that covered Boston, Amherst/ North Hampton, Hartford, New York, Philadelphia, DC, Atlanta, Cleveland, Chicago, and Detroit. He also got a couple of gigs in Canada (Montreal and Ontario). For the tour, Yusef stripped down the band to himself on keyboards, his old buddy Barry on bass, Clement (who was back from his world tour) on sax and flute, a drummer and a drum machine. The band boarded a rented, rehabbed Grumman's bus and away they went. Their road manager, Allan, was also a filmmaker. While they were on the road, Allan was going to capture footage of the band playing gigs and various other shots with his supper 8mm camera. He would later cut the footage into a music video for the record. They knew that MTV wouldn't play it, but all of the local and public access video programs would.

*****

Clement sat at the little round table in the hotel room, eating fried chicken, greens, and black-eyed peas from an aluminum container purchased at a soul-food joint around the corner from the club they played in on U Street. The tour had been in swing for about a week and a half. Yusef was in the shower getting ready for a night on the town. The gig that night was over by 11 PM, so Yusef, Barry and the drummer were going to experience some of DC's local nightlife. Clement, on the other hand, was settling in for an evening of *Nick At Night* and bed. Three months on a world tour taught him how to pace himself. The next morning, they had a live radio performance at an NPR station, Yusef had an in-store promo appearance in the afternoon, and they had another show at the same club that night. They would be in North Carolina the night after for another show, with more radio and store appearances. An all-night bus ride to Atlanta would follow.

*****

Yusef looked out of his hotel window thinking of Dizzy Gillespie's, *I'll Never Go Back To Georgia*. Of course, Gillespie's Atlanta wasn't the "Chocolate City" that it was now. "Awwwww yeah. Yusef, you always had good timing with things, but Freaknik? Yeah, man!" Barry excitedly mused, "Girls everywhere... clubs, streets, beaches... everywhere bumping with music and folks. This is the time to have a gig and a record out." Of course this gig wasn't set up by chance. Atif knew that this was the time to be in Atlanta to pump a new record. They made up a cassette E.P. of four tunes, handing them out to folks with loud car stereo systems. *Valley Park Groove* became the club record of choice and their gigs were jammed-packed with college kids trying to look like sophisticated jazz lovers. By the end of Freaknik, several thousand copies of *Valley Park Groove* left in the car stereos and bags of college kids heading back to their respective campuses, spreading Yusef's music like a virus.

*****

At the sound check, the band couldn't help but to play the theme song from "Good Times." I mean, damn, they *were* playing a club in Chicago. Frankie Knuckles had been invited to the gig. Atif personally sent him a test pressing back in January and, to his understanding, Frankie had been playing Valley Park Groove" at his sets.

Melodic Reprise:
September 1990 – New York City

Yusef, Atif and Sandra sat on the twelfth floor of 52 West 51st Street, in the office of the head A&R person of the company's dance music division. "*Valley Park Groove* can be the next biggest instrumental dance hit since Paul Hardcastle's *Rain Forest*," she excitedly told the trio. As she spoke, Yusef thought back to almost a year ago when this same woman turned the track down cold, saying that it didn't fit in with what people wanted to hear these days. Now, she was praising it like it was genius. Praise from a major label might have turned his head at one point; but now, the bottom line was this: *What could a major label do for them, financially, that they could not do for themselves?* The three of them had a label, investors, and a hit record. Yusef and his band had just spent the summer playing in England, Germany, and France. Liberation Records had a deal with a label in England to release the cut in Europe. Between record sales, gigs, and publishing, the only thing that the major label could offer was more exposure and maybe more money. Of course, the overhead costs that labels stick onto the artist's expense sheet always eat up most of the income from sales. Over the next couple of days, it was the same story at three other major labels.

Yusef thought about the deal. All they wanted was distribution, like Russell Simmons got for Def Jam back in the 1980's, but the majors wanted to outright sign the Bass Mint Brothers to an album deal. Not having the Liberation label involved in the record if he went to a major, would also kill the chances of the record having the proper promotion and marketing behind it. Majors didn't know or really understand these niche markets and they were getting too arrogant to admit it. As far as they were concerned, if your record was a hit, they'd make money; if your record was a flop, they could write it off and make money. As Yusef and Sandra made the drive back up to Boston, Yusef's head swam as he thought about contracts, options, rights, recoupable losses, promotion costs, and first right refusals. All he wanted to do was play his music, make a record, and gig. His mind went back to the days of making music on Atif's four-track and drumming in the park with his father. He thought about those long nights in the studio and the rush that all of it gave him... Most of all Yusef just thought, as the car rolled up I-95. Thanks to summer courses and a practicum at the Roland Hayes School, he'd be able to finish his master's degree by September 1991.

The words of the Dance Music A&R person at the major, rang in his ears, "Very few people have opportunities like this handed to them. This could be really big!" As they passed through Connecticut, the late night DJ on U. Conn's station started to play "Valley Park Groove." Yusef switched off the radio. "So, tell me more about independent distribution and marketing..." he said to Sandra with a smile. She was thinking the same thing. After all, the label was called "Liberation."

Outro:
Present Day – Bronx, NY

At about 3:30 PM, on a crisp autumn day, Yusef waited for the Two Train at 180th Street. He was on his way to engineer a session at the studio for a dance hall artist. As the train rolled and rattled down the tracks, Yusef began to think about a melody that came to him in a dream. Most of his melodic ideas came to him in dreams, leaving him to find the harmony himself. It was like a puzzle. There in the station, the melody started to come to him; but, it was interrupted by the clamor of three kids, appearing to be between 14 and 15 years old, who came walking up the stairs to the train platform. He noticed that two of them were carrying musical instruments. The third one, a short, dark-skinned kid with his hair in twists, had a large, leather artist's portfolio in his hand. They strolled down the platform and stood, leaning on the wall, close to were Yusef waited. They were talking and laughing, as most kids on their way to school. One kid held a saxophone case, was very neatly dressed and wore round, wire-rimmed glasses. The kid was tallish, almond-colored, and skinny. The faint line over his lip, which would one day become a moustache, looked as though the young man had spent hours in front of the mirror trying to trim it just right. The third wore a LaGuardia jacket and carried what looked like a viola case. He was stocky and also dressed neatly, but in an unkempt sort of way.

"So, he put you in the jazz band?" the kid with the sax mused.

"Yeah, I had to buy a pick-up and an amp so that I could be heard." responded the kid with the viola.

"That's gonna be fat! Are you going to use any of the effects pedals?" asked the kid with the art portfolio.

"Maybe later. I should get used to the natural sound first."

"What did you audition for him with?" asked the kid with the sax.

"I played 'Yard Bird' and ran a few improv. lines."

"Are you gonna get one of those fancy electric violas? I saw one down on 48th Street in that shop near Sam Ash."

"Naw, my teacher said they're poorly made. She wasn't too up on me doing the jazz thing in the first place. To me, the classics were getting kinda boring."

"What do your parents think?"

"My dad is all for it. My mom was like 'at least he practices more now...'."

"Have you ever seen him practice on his improv?" asked the kid with the portfolio.

"Naw." responded the kid with the sax.

"He turns on the radio, puts it on almost any station, and plays off of the music. He was jammin' offa WBLS the other night. I wish I had it on tape."

Their conversation moved towards a discussion about some female dance student's butt. Yusef smiled to himself, thinking about how everything goes in cycles. These three kids were just like he, Atif, and Clement were almost 25 years before.

*****

In Ann Arbor, Michigan there is a used record store that specializes in old vinyl. There, you can find tons of old Motown 45s in mint condition. Encased in a glass counter, you can find really rare and classic records for sale. Among the vintage records is a copy of "Valley Park Groove". It sells for $20. "Vintage Liberation Release" read the store's tag over the record.

... Atif and Yusef had been sitting back on a Sunday afternoon in their Dale Street apartment, sipping wine and listening to some new records that had come in from the record pool.

~ Fifteen ~

A RETURN TO THE BACKWOODS
A PARADISE REBORN

The story continues,
or repeats,
or skips back and forth;
it really doesn't matter, 'cause
IT'S ALL THE SAME AND IT'S ALL GOOD, IN THE BACKWOODS!!!

They say that everything must change. Now, don't ask me who 'they" is, 'cause that really doesn't matter. The issue that I'm addressing is the "change" factor. Does *everything* really change? If everything changes, then to what extent does it change? I mean, in the Backwoods they say that nothing changes. That's right, *nothing changes*. Especially if you overlook such minor details as older folks remembering the introduction of electricity and indoor plumbing, and folk being born (or dying...). Of course, it always seems that when somebody is born and grows up, they always seem to remind the elders of somebody who used to be around. I guess if you take that into account, things don't really change, they just repeat with a slight variation – kinda like a jazz tune.

For years, folks who weren't from the Backwoods would occasionally pass through the Backwoods on trips and vacations. Often, these visitors and "passers-through" would leave their mark in some way – like the way a mosquito does when it bites you. You see, folks from out of town have a tendency to act like everything in the Backwoods is there for their amusement, even the people. Visitors like to talk about Backwoods people like they're not really there. They also like to use terms like "quaint" and "primitive" to describe what they see. If you're from the Backwoods, don't be too surprised if somebody suddenly pops up and takes a picture of you doing some *quaintly primitive* Backwoods activity or doing nothing but standing against a *quaint* Backwoods landscape.

Backwoods folks never seem to mind too much, but it's really just their passive aggressive streaks showing. Backwoods folks love to tell these visitors outrageous stories about local legends; like the tale of the man whose leg got cut off while he was chopping wood one moonless night, and how even since then, the leg can still be heard hopping through the forests and swamps on moonless nights. When visitors whip out their cameras, some Backwoods folks will do all kinds of outrageous things. There was the time that this Backwoods kid was fishing in the millpond and some visitors driving by thought it was *quaint* so they stopped to take a picture. The kid acted like he didn't notice them, but just before the woman snapped the picture, the Backwoods kid threw a fish in their car. Aside from the fact that their car had cloth seats, neither of them knew what to do with a live, flopping fish; nor did they have any idea of how to get it out of the car. What else could you expect from one of those *primitive* little Backwoods bad-asses?

Another time some visitors pulled up to the Backwoods store because they thought the sight of two *primitive* looking Backwoods men standing there having a conversation was also *quaint*. One of the men asked if the visitor's wife would like to get in the picture with them, and she agreed. The wife, finding this all so *quaintly* amusing, stood between the two men with a hand on each of their shoulders. One of the Backwoods men told the visitor with the camera to take the picture on his count... *1, 2, 3 – FLASH!!!* The visitor got a really nice picture of the two grinning Backwoods men lifting his wife's skirt from either side, blocking her out of the picture all together.... except for her legs and underwear. The visitor with the camera saw the humor in the situation, or at least pretended to – as he was not about to tangle with two Backwoods men. The wife, however, was outraged. *How could people objectify another human being like that?* Some Backwoods folks dream of a day when a bunch of them will get on a bus and go into these visitor's neighborhoods and take pictures of *them*; but for now, IT'S ALL THE SAME AND IT'S ALL GOOD, IN THE BACKWOODS!!!

I've said it before, but just for emphasis; there is little in the way of race prejudice in the Backwoods. In the Backwoods, you have people with brown eyes, blue eyes, gray eyes, green eyes, hazel eyes, brown hair, black hair, red hair, blonde hair, dark skin, light skin, brown skin, straight hair, curly hair, kinky hair, no hair... and this could all be in one family. For the folks from the Frontwoods and the Nowoods, these differences are grounds for all kinds of problems, but not in the Backwoods. That was, of course, until outsiders began moving into the Backwoods, trying to get back to nature; and of course, they had their own ideas about how to 'improve" on nature so that the Backwoods would be a little more livable.

I'm not sure if I mentioned this before, but Backwoods people love themselves some guns. I should also point out that they hunt for food and skins and not simply for sport. Anyplace where there are animals is a place to go hunting, even if that place happens to be a neighbor's backyard. Of course, as long as you don't shoot your neighbor or their family, and you share some of the game– it's all good in the Backwoods. Eventually, some Frontwoods folks moved to town and got really nervous about these Backwoods people running around with guns, especially the darker-skinned ones with kinky hair. For some reason, they didn't find the idea of them having guns as so *quaint*. Frontwoods folks would be out taking nature walks or walking their dogs and would get really bent out of shape when the occasional Backwoods hunter would pop out of the woods on the trail of some deer, possum, or raccoon. Of course, this, not to mention the notion of taking your dog for a walk, amused Backwoods people. Backwoods dogs were allowed to roam freely 'cause they'd always come home when they were called. The idea of keeping a dog in the house all day, then taking them out on a leash seemed ridiculous. It almost seemed as ridiculous as having to keep explaining to some screaming fool who threw their wallet at your feet that you were just out hunting. The notion of Backwoods people trying to steal from a person was ridiculous and insulting. Hell, why would folks need to steal? If you need something, just ask for it and somebody'll give it to you. That's just the way it is in the Backwoods.

One weekend, a group of hunters got together and formed "The Sportsman's Club." This was an effort to make the newcomers more comfortable, as well as, to keep the Backwoods police station from getting so many hysterical phone calls. They reasoned that these hair-brained newcomers would feel more relaxed about seeing folks with guns if they also wore jackets with an emblem on it. Then, the hunters built themselves a clubhouse – a nice little "home away from home" – where they could relax after a day of hunting… or just get out of the house. Sometimes, the members would gather to play cards; talk about sports, politics, current events in town, the weather, good spots for fishing, argue about the best time to prune apple and pear trees; they'd have dinners and family events… yeah, the Backwoods hunters had their own little place to hang their guns, hats, and game for dressing.

A Mixed Medicine Bag

With each generation, there was always an elder among the hunters who became the de facto patriarch of the group. In this generation, the de facto patriarch was a guy who seemed particularly unpleasant, but was really the kindest of people. If you asked him to do something, he would grumble, mumble, and possibly even curse you out, but he would do what ever you asked – within reason. (Note: Backwoods folks have a different list of what's reasonable, compared to most folks you might know). His general philosophical answer to all of life's issues was "the sun still rises." This elder was also an exceptionally good cook, often serving as the cook for the club's dinners and impromptu meetings (card games, watching football games together, etc.). Even though it was the club's kitchen, all of the members regarded it as the elder's kitchen. The club also had one female member; she was the club's secretary. She took her job very seriously, insisting that during meetings, members would conduct themselves in a business-like fashion. This meant no cursing or consumption of distilled spirits during the meetings. No one in the club appreciated this policy, but they weren't going to argue on account of the fact that she did keep good notes, not to mention was the best shot in the room.

Law enforcement was never a big issue in the Backwoods. I mean it was a job with good pay, so why not be a cop? But generally, beyond a few harsh words, fights, or the need to protect a stray Backwoods husband from the wrath of his wife, nothing much really happened. The force had four cops: A chief, a dispatcher, and two shifts. All four of them were related, but only two of them could explain how. The night shift had only one cop. Since very little happened in the Backwoods, the night patrolman usually ended up driving around town, listening to the radio, napping, and collecting dropped wallets in the parking lot of the local dance hall after closing (he supplemented his income by an average of $130 a week). One night, while the Backwoods patrolman was collecting lost wallets, one of the biggest crimes ever took place. You see, while it was not unusual for Backwoods folks to enjoy sipping Backwoods distilled spirits every now and again, some folks acted like this was their occupation and were called "town drunks". On this night, one of the more ambitious town drunks decided to do some shopping at the package (liquor) store, using an axe to get in through the back wall. He made off with a case of gin, but was soon caught (he'd left footprints through the woods that led to his back porch). Rather then sending him to jail, the judge ordered him to repair the wall and to perform landscaping duties around town hall for the next five months. While performing his community service, the drunk discovered that he had talents in both carpentry and landscaping – thus, a new career. That's rehabilitation Backwoods-style.

Most Backwoods people liked to stay in the Backwoods. But every now and again you'll have somebody from the Backwoods who might decide to move out and see the world. They'll go off to school or just for adventure; but sometimes this wasn't voluntary. You see, for some reason the government never seemed to know where or what the Backwoods were when it was a matter of the Backwoods people being in need. However, when it came to the armed forces, they always seemed to be able to find Backwoods people first. As a result, you have many Backwoods men who have been world travelers, having seen the most interesting places. On account of their proficiency with guns, the armed forces always seemed to like Backwoods men. Those who survived the armed forces (it seems that their leaders would sometimes want them to do the dumbest things) returned with the most amazing stories to tell their families and friends. They told tales about being decorated war heroes, learning new card games, folks they met, or being locked in the stockade for using an army-issued gun for hunting.

Leaving the Backwoods was almost always a case of culture shock because most Backwoods people ended up having to live in the Nowoods. Moving to the Frontwoods (known to some as the "suburbs") would have probably been less of shock, but as life has it, folks would have to live and work in the Nowoods for quite a while before they could afford to live in the Frontwoods. Anyway, some Backwoods folks who moved to the Nowoods stayed a while and even started families. They would bring their families to the Backwoods for visits and, unfortunately, their Nowoods children would become the source of a lot of amusement for their Backwoods relatives. These particular Nowoods children were the first generation to be born outside of the Backwoods, and were not used to the sounds of the Backwoods at night. The first night of their visit was always the same: jumping every time they heard a rabbit hopping, the wind in the trees, the screen door creaking, and so forth. Their Backwoods cousins didn't help matters; they'd tell stories to their Nowoods kin about ghosts, headless bodies, bodiless heads, and a strange leg that hops around the woods on moonless nights (all lurking in the woods – waiting for strangers). Then, they would ditch their Nowoods cousins in the woods around sunset to find their own way home. The Nowoods cousins weren't used to walking on the sides of roads; they kept looking for a sidewalk. They also wore fancy bathing suits when they went swimming (instead of cut-off shorts). I won't even go into the funny way that the Nowoods cousins talked... those accents... and slang terms... they were a hoot!

Then came a day when it was a Backwoods cousin's turn to visit the Nowoods for a few weeks. He'd heard all kinds of stories about the Nowoods that made it sound like quite an exciting place. In reality, it was like the Fresh Air Fund... in reverse. His family took him to the bus station approximately two towns away. Since anytime anyone went into the Nowoods it was an important occasion, when he got to the station, half of the Backwoods was there to see him off. The trip took about seven hours – which felt like forever – but finally, the bus pulled into the Nowoods; passing big buildings, busy streets with traffic and people going in every direction. Lights and lights and lights... lights were everywhere, and stores, and people selling stuff on the streets – some from trays, stands, and their jacket pockets. The bus pulled into the Nowoods Port Authority and his No-Backwoods uncle and Nowoods cousins greeted the Backwoods youth.

As they walked through the Port Authority to the uncle's Nowood Vehicle (an SUV)... I know, you're wondering why somebody would need an SUV in the city. Have you ever seen some of those streets? The Nowoods cousins fed him stories of crazy people, gangs, crooks, thugs, and other perils that existed in their apartment building alone. The No-Backwoods uncle had a funny little box on his key ring that made the car beep when he pressed it. He also had a big steel bar on the steering wheel with a big lock on it. Getting into his car was like going into the vault of a bank. In the Backwoods, not only did people leave their cars unlocked, but a lot of folks left their car keys in the car. The Backwoods cousin got to see a lot from the car window as the car had to stop at traffic lights every few feet, it seemed. Back in the Backwoods, they had miles and miles of roads with maybe only two traffic lights, if you counted the blinker. They had to park about a quarter of a mile (Uncle called it five blocks) from their apartment building.

The Backwoods cousin noticed all of these grubby folks sitting and laying around the streets. He figured that these must have been the Nowoods Town Drunks. As they passed one sitting in front of the neighborhood store, one of the NTD asked him for a quarter. The Backwoods cousin reached in his pocket and pulled out a dollar and gave it to the NTD. Heck he was grubby and a drunk and all, but he was still a person. Welcome to the Nowoods.

The building was quite a sight. It was six stories tall and had a big, glass entry way like the one at the mall. The Backwoods youth asked if this was what they called a high-rise tower. His cousins laughed as their father explained that there were buildings with fifty and sixty stories, in comparison, this was no high-rise. The building had this teeny, tiny backyard that couldn't have been a sixteenth of an acre. It had a tall fence around it that separated it from a bunch of other yards that looked the same. The basement and first floor had steel mesh on the windows and the second and third floors had gates that moved across the windows. The Backwoods cousin figured that moving to the Nowoods must have been a lot like going to the state jail.

If you recall, Backwoods people came in all shapes, sizes, colors, and so forth; it was not unusual for a chocolate brown woman to have a brother who was blonde and blue-eyed. Well this seemed to be the basis of a lot of separation in the Nowoods. Neighborhoods were defined mostly by what folks living there looked like. Case in point, they had some Backwoods cousins who were blonde and blue-eyed who lived in another part of town and tried to pretend that they didn't even know these uptown, Nowoods cousins.

It came to be time for bed and of course, it was all too loud and exciting for the Backwoods cousin to get any sleep. They had street lights that stayed on all night long, cars, horns, alarms, screaming people, sirens, gunshots, and radios. One day they went to this big park in the middle of the Nowoods, where the Backwoods cousin could see that they had all kinds of game living in the park. Judging from the tracks that they left in the dirt, there were foxes, beavers, raccoons, rabbits, squirrels, possums, skunks, and a few kinds of hawks living in this concrete world. When he pointed this out to his cousins and their friends, they all just looked at him like he was crazy until their No-Backwoods father agreed.

In the uptown part of the Nowoods they had a lot of package stores, bars, and prayer meeting houses. There seemed to be one or the other of them on almost every corner. They also had neighborhood stores that were kinda like the store in the town center back home. Their stores had red and yellow, plastic awnings and the shopkeepers were no nonsense business people, like the shopkeeper back home; except they spoke in funny accents and sometimes even different languages. One day, the Backwoods cousin bought a bag of what he thought were potato chips, except they were thicker and sweeter and looked like banana slices. They were really good.

Nowoods people loved themselves some guns, but it seemed they never used them for hunting. In fact, it seemed that the folks who did the most talking about guns were the biggest cowards in the group (like the guns gave them a feeling of power or something). The Backwoods cousin felt really uneasy when he realized that all of those gun shots he would hear were not night hunters like at home, but people shooting at each other (like they did in the bar back home that time that everybody talks about). This is not to say that folks at home didn't do dumb stuff with guns once in a while, but they usually caught hold of their senses once they were subdued by the rest of the community.

One night, the Nowoods cousins and their friends took the Backwoods cousin to a party. On their way home, some Nowoods punk rolled up on them with his hand in his coat, demanding their money and watches. The Backwoods cousin grabbed the punk's arms and pinned him to the ground. He knew the punk didn't have a gun, because he knew that the guy wasn't going to blow a hole in that nice leather jacket the punk was wearing... Some folks would say that the Backwoods cousin mugged the punk for his coat, but it was really just a lesson: You don't play with folks from the Backwoods. For the rest of his visit, the Nowoods cousins and their friends regarded the Backwoods cousin with certain deference, if not respect.

The Backwoods cousin finally returned home, where he sat on the steps of the Backwoods store, the way Nowoods folks gather on the fronts of their buildings, stores, and barbershops, and told the tale of his adventures in the Nowoods (as they admired his fancy leather jacket). He even asked the shopkeeper if he could see about carrying those funny little banana chips – they were good. He talked of how folks in the city got really mad if you shot at game in the parks or backyards. In the Nowoods, it's called "Reckless endangerment with a deadly weapon." Here, IT'S ALL THE SAME, AND IT'S ALL GOOD, IN THE BACKWOODS!!!!

I'm going to skip a few years and a few tales about how the Backwoods cousin ended up going to the same college as his Nowoods cousins. I'll even skip past the story about the No-Backwoods uncle who decided to retire to the Backwoods, buying his grandmother's house and property. We don't need to talk about how the uncle grew a garden with tomatoes, joined the sportsman's club, went hunting and fishing with his family and friends, and even helped a cousin rebuild his kitchen (...another story in itself.). I think I'll jump to his two boys graduating from college and feeling like aliens in the Backwoods. Even their cousin lost a little of his Backwoods edge while in school. College left them all with a social and political consciousness that was a little too radical for the Backwoods elders. This happened to a lot of young folks who went away to college and came home to the Backwoods to be some of the best educated hunters, fishermen, landscapers, and associate shopkeepers in the Backwoods. To some of you, this might seem like a major disappointment, but around here IT'S ALL THE SAME AND IT'S ALL GOOD, IN THE BACKWOODS!!!

They also noticed that the Backwoods was changing, and growing, with a way of life being squashed out. The three cousins took to hanging out together a lot, sitting in each other's basements long into the night, talking. They joined the Sportsman's Club and hung out in Backwoods nightclubs on the weekends; the particular one that they used to hang out in during summer breaks was now a strip club. All week, they worked really hard at jobs that had nothing to do with what they studied. They started out renting a house down the street from their parents. Their landlord eventually put the house on the market; so they pooled their money and bought it. The back property line abutted several Frontwoods folks, a couple of whom tried to urge the elderly landlord not to sell the house to young folks, but the landlord knew the boys to be from a good, Backwoods family. The three cousins promptly built a fence along their property line, which one Frontwoods neighbor deemed inconsiderate, as it blocked her view of their trees.

Over the next several months, the trio did renovation work on the house. Some of the things they did became the talk of the town: putting in a satellite dish, moving a whole lot of computer equipment into the house, building long green houses in the backyard, and the weirdest of all, putting a big windmill in the backyard with funny looking glass and shiny aluminum panels on the roof. They took a real teasing at the Sportsman's Club, where the elder asked them if they were going to start wearing wooden shoes. Some of them even came by and asked about the apparatus – how it worked (and how they could get something like it for their house).

A Mixed Medicine Bag

Backwoods men have the ability to tease you and admire what you're doing all at the same time.

Eventually, the country fell into economic collapse, which seemed to affect everybody in the backwoods except the Backwoods people. Like when there was a sudden, sharp increase in the price of groceries, Backwoods people had gardens and, in the words of one Backwoods elder, "Well, ya got guns, ain'tcha? Better meat in the woods than that stuff in the stores anyway... don't have all of them chemicals in it."

The newspapers were carrying all kinds of stories about serious budget cuts to education, human services, and so forth; but there was nothing really new about that. They reported that giant corporations were swallowing up smaller companies in mergers; but, there was nothing really new about that, either. In fact, all it meant was that folks would be getting new checkbooks, with new names, from their same old banks... again.

Suddenly, utility costs began to skyrocket and a lot of Backwoods folks began having their gas and electricity shut off in favor of the windmills they had installed in their yards, and solar panels that they had installed on their roofs. Folks also began going back to using their old wells and pumps instead of town water.

A lot of folks from the Frontwoods and Nowoods began to move out of the Backwoods, selling their homes and businesses rather cheaply. In fact, a lot of Backwoods families were able to repurchase their grandparent's properties for next to nothing; which is only fair since they originally sold it for next to nothing, or had it taken from them. Other newcomers began abandoning their homes. It seems that without money from their investments in those big corporations that folded, they had nothing to keep them going out in the Backwoods. Some Backwoods people moved into the big houses that the outsiders left behind. Some folks knocked down a few of the houses to allow the plants and trees to take over the land once again. They even let a couple of the big, fancy golf courses revert to wetlands and swamps. Now, with a serious population dip and fewer houses, the Backwoods looked the way it did when the oldest of the living elders were children.

The restoration of the Backwoods was a hot topic among the folks at the Sportsman's Club meeting, along with arguments about good times to prune apple and pear trees. The elder of the club just sat there, sipping Backwoods distilled spirits, and smoking a cigarette until he finally said, "the sun still rises." You see; he understood that anything created had to be maintained. Nature creates and is able to sustain what it creates 'cause nature is going to be here forever. Greedy people and the things they create will never last for very long 'cause greedy people are usually also rather lazy. There were times in the past that greedy people tried to erase the Backwoods, but it always ended that the Backwoods erased them. After all – it *is* the Backwoods.

Yep, everything had gone back to the way it used to be in the Backwoods. Well, okay, a few things kinda changed. For one thing, on occasion, groups of Backwoods women would disappear for the weekend on hunting and fishing trips, leaving the Backwoods men at home with the children. One weekend, the men built a small playground at the Sportsman's Club where they would gather on the weekends with their children; or you'd find them in their backyards tending to their vegetable gardens.

To some folks, it seems like the Backwoods never changes; but in reality, everything changes. It's just that Backwoods people adapt to the world around them. When the world is technologically advanced, the Backwoods people adapt, just like they would when the technology wasn't there. However, even when Backwoods folks adapt, they do it in their own *special* way. Either way, as long as the sun still rises, IT'S ALL THE SAME AND IT'S ALL GOOD, IN THE BACKWOODS!!!

* Backwoods, Frontwoods, and Nowoods are capitalized because they are ethno-cultural identities, like African, Native American, Latino, European, etc.

The Sun Still Rises.

MWALIM
Morgan James Peters, I

Mwalim (Morgan James Peters, I) is an award winning, Mashpee Wampanoag performing artist, writer, and educator. A master storyteller, his body of work includes many plays, stories, performance pieces, essays, poems, articles, and musical compositions. Growing up immersed in the oral traditions of his Black and Northeastern Native American heritages, Mwalim is a keeper of both the New World Griot and Wampanoag Ahanaeenun (Clown) traditions. His body of work is a rich blend of humor, folk-wisdom, and social commentary. As a performer, his stages have included theatres, coffeehouses, powwows, festivals, nightclubs, colleges, museums, schools, jails, temples, libraries, and street corners throughout the USA and Canada. He is a recording artist on Midnight Groove Records.

Mwalim has been an artist-in-residence and lecturer at arts and educational institutions throughout the eastern United States. An Assistant Professor of English and African/ African American Studies at the University of Massachusetts Dartmouth, his *Black Folklore & Aesthetics* course is one of the most popular classes on campus. Mwalim is a playwright-in-residence at New African Company in Boston, and a Historian for the Prince Hall Grand Lodge of Massachusetts. He is a past recipient of the Longwood Cyber Artist Fellowship, the New York Theatre Forum's "Outstanding New Playwright" award, and a three-time recipient of the Ira Aldridge Fellowship. Mwalim earned his BA in Music and MS in Film from Boston University as well as an MFA from Goddard College. Mwalim currently lives in the National Wampanoag Territory (Southeastern Massachusetts) with his son, Zyggi.

www.mwalim.com

Mwalim *7)